Nothing Wrong
with a
Three-Legged Dog

Nothing Wrong with a Three-Legged Dog

Graham McNamee

A YEARLING BOOK

35 Years of Exceptional Reading

Yearling Books
Established 1966

Published by
Dell Yearling
an imprint of
Random House Children's Books
a division of Random House, Inc.
1540 Broadway
New York, New York 10036

Visit us on the Web! www.randomhouse.com/kids

Educators and librarians, for a variety of teaching tools, visit us at www.randomhouse.com/teachers

ISBN: 0-440-41687-6

Reprinted by arrangement with Delacorte Press

Printed in the United States of America

August 2001

10 9 8 7 6 5 4 3 2 1

OPM

For Cadet Stimpy and Bobo
old buddies, best pals

One

My name is Keath. But you can call me Whitey. Or Vanilla. Or Mayonnaise. Whatever.

At school they mostly call me Whitey. My best friend is Lynda. Some call her Zebra, which is kind of a nice name, only the kids who say it mean it in a bad way.

Lynda is Zebra because her mother is black and her father is white.

Real zebras are beautiful. They're these African horses painted white with black stripes, and they have Mohawk hair that runs from the top of their head down their neck and stands up straight. So Lynda says when they call her Zebra she thinks about the horse with the Mohawk, and the name doesn't burn so bad.

We're both ten. We go to Frederick Douglass, which is a pretty good school. It's downtown. There aren't too many white kids; I'm the only one in my fourth-grade class.

At lunch in the cafeteria I'm sitting with Lynda when Toothpick and Blob pass by. Toothpick is Toothpick because he's tall and thin, all skin and sharp pointy bones. I've seen him fight and he's like a porcupine: you try to wrestle him and you're jabbed by an elbow or a knee or kicked with a needle-sharp heel. It's like he's got a giant electric bone sharpener at home he sticks his fingers and elbows and knees in before bed, while other kids are busy brushing their teeth.

"Hey, White Bread," Toothpick calls me.

I drag a limp french fry through a puddle of gravy on my plate.

"Talking to you, Whitey."

I have to look up sooner or later. He's never going to just leave. I shoot a look over at Lynda, who's staring at her Jell-O cubes.

"What kind of sandwich you got there? May-o-naise sandwich?" Toothpick says.

Blob snorts. Blob is Blob because he's big—not just fat big but *big* big. It's always weird to see this huge guy tagging along after a skinny sliver. Toothpick's in charge because he's meaner. Mean beats big the way a needle busts a balloon.

I'm thinking all this so I don't have to think about Toothpick's pointy knuckles.

He's totally in my face now with his needle nose.

I stare him in the eye. Dad always says choose one eye on a person and stare at it, then you don't look so shifty and scared.

"Yes," I say. "It's a white bread mayonnaise vanilla honky sandwich."

Out of the edge of the corner of my eye that's still staring straight at Toothpick, I can see Lynda's smiling at that.

It makes the whack in the back of the head I know is coming to me worth it.

Wham!

I see sparks for a few seconds. I try to blink them away.

"What are you smiling at, Zebra?" Toothpick says. "I still got some left for you."

I try to stand and block him from getting to Lynda but it's like my legs are pretzels, all twisted.

"Last call," the lunch lady shouts out. "I'm closing up."

"Come on," Blob says. "I need some fries."

Toothpick, who's leaning over Lynda now, picks up a blue Jell-O cube. He pinches it so it splits open and he takes out the grape that was inside.

Popping the grape in his mouth, he drops the Jell-O pieces back on her plate.

"Right," he says to Blob. "Fries."

When they're gone my legs slowly un-pretzel and the sparks fade.

"I wonder what a white bread mayonnaise vanilla honky sandwich would taste like, anyhow," Lynda laughs. "Good one."

I rub the back of my head. Yeah, it was worth it.

Two

The first time I saw Lynda she was carrying a shopping bag full of dog turds.

I had just gotten out of detention. I was sentenced to two hours' detention for fighting, and I didn't even fight back, just got punched.

This kid named Ryan, the only kid in class who's shorter than me, bumped into me in the hall and started arguing. I didn't know what was going on.

"I'm just standing here," I said. "How can I bump you if I'm not even moving?"

He got this puzzled look. Then he told me, "Shut up," and right there by the drinking fountain he jumped me. Ryan got one hard shot in before a teacher pulled him off.

Later on, my pal Hairy Larry explained it to me.

"This is how I figure it. Ryan's like the runt of the class," Larry told me. "You're the only one he had a chance at beating in a fight. So I guess he got tired of being the lowest worm on the food chain. Now he's second to last."

"That's crazy," I said. "I've never done nothing to him."

Larry just shrugged. "It's not really like he was mad at you. It's just that now Ryan probably won't get smacked around so much—I mean, he's still a runt, but he's not last anymore."

"So now I'm the lowest worm?" I said.

"You the worm, man."

"Great." I just shook my head. "How did you figure all this out?"

Hairy Larry tapped his forehead. "Psychic. No, I cornered Ryan and asked him why he hit you and he said, 'Because he let me.' "

You know, I've been going to this school forever, and it never used to be this bad. But when Toothpick moved in, things started to change.

So anyway, I still had a bruise on my cheek when I met Lynda holding the dog doodles. She was walking behind a man with nine leashes, surrounded by dogs of every size and hairstyle.

I stopped and stared. To stand waist deep in a crowd of dogs, that's my idea of Heaven.

When I grow up I want to be a golden retriever.

My dad's allergic to dogs and cats and everything furry so I'm totally petless.

Mom got me a giant cactus for my room. If you look at it with the lights turned off it looks like it's in a holdup, like someone with their hands in the air. Mom goes shopping in the Twilight Zone. I mean, what do you do with a cactus? It doesn't fetch or even roll over, at least not without a lot of help.

I'm telling you all this so you'll understand how dogs are my destiny—just like how Darth Vader tells Luke, "It is your destiny!" Except I'm talking pooches.

Lynda saw me staring at her dogs. She pointed at my bruise.

"I saw that fight," she told me. "Looked real painful."

"Yeah." I rubbed my cheek as if the bruise would come off and I wouldn't look like such a loser. "What's in the bag?"

She made a face with her nose. "Poop. I'm on poop alert. They poop, I scoop."

I followed her following the dogs.

"Those all your dogs?" I asked.

"No." She pointed. "That's my dad. He's a dog walker." Lynda tossed a full poop bag in a trash bin.

"Wow. Is that a job? I mean, you get paid to do that?" I said.

"It's not a real real job. My mom's a veterinarian—that's a real real job. But Dad gets paid to exercise these dogs and take care of them during the day when their owners are at work."

I've got dog books at home that name all the different kinds. On the nine leashes there were retrievers, black and golden; three terriers that didn't even come up to my knees; a Doberman; a collie; a poodle wearing a blue sweater; and a beagle that walked funny.

"That beagle's sort of limping." I pointed him out to Lynda.

"That's Leftovers. He's my dog. Come on over and let him smell you."

Leftovers was one sad-looking dog. His back left leg was gone, totally gone, with just a stump where it should have been. Instead of walking like the other dogs, Leftovers kind of bounced along.

"Leftovers," Lynda called to him. "Come here, bunny. Come on, make friends."

The beagle made his way through the pack. We crouched down to say hello.

Leftovers lunged at me, burying his head in my crotch and nearly knocking me over.

"He's saying hello," Lynda told me.

Leftovers finished his inspection and gave me a full-tongue lick all over my neck up to my chin. I could feel his drool dripping from my Adam's apple, the grossest, most amazing feeling.

I was petting his head, scratching him behind his ears, when one of them came off in my hand. I gasped and stared down at it.

Leftovers sniffed at the ear and started chewing on it.

"Don't worry," Lynda said. "That's always coming loose. It's not his real ear. See?" She rubbed it between her fingers. "It's just leather. He lost his real ear when he lost his leg. Got hit by a car."

My heart started beating again. What a shock! It's like shaking someone's hand and coming away with a few of their fingers.

"He really *is* leftovers," I said.

"Don't eat!" Lynda told the beagle, pulling the leather out of his mouth.

She said, "See how the fake ear fits like a glove over the stump left over from his real ear? Beagles have these droopy ears, so without it everything sounds super loud, and Leftovers gets nervous and jumpy."

Lynda slipped the ear back on. The beagle rejoined the pack with his weird bouncing walk. Every streetlamp, hydrant and newspaper box got fully sniffed by the crowd and peed on (their stamp of approval).

Lynda's father saw me following and asked, "Who's your friend?"

"Don't know," Lynda said. "He's in my class at school. They call him Whitey."

"Whitey?" her father said. "Does he have a name?"

"Don't know," Lynda said, turning to me. "Do you?"

"Keath. Keath Fraser. They call me Whitey."

"Yeah?" he said. "Well, I'll call you Keath. You want to help Lynda? How about fifty cents for every poop you scoop?"

I shook my head. "I'll do it for free."

He laughed. "You must be a dog lover too." He bent down to untangle the terriers. "Watch out, Keath. This is what doggie love gets you: a mountain of poop and a whole lot of drool."

That's how I met Lynda and Leftovers and fell in love. With Leftovers, I mean, not Lynda. She's okay, but she's no beagle.

Three

At breakfast I try eating some Froot Loops dry, without chewing. That's how snakes eat. They just swallow and their stomach muscles grind the bones up inside.

It doesn't work with Froot Loops. They go down my throat real scratchy and tasteless.

Dad sees the face I'm making. "Try chewing," he says, shaking his head.

Dad's got his work uniform on. He's a security guard at the Chrysler Building. He makes sure no one steals it. That's a joke.

"They had this thing at school yesterday—The Reptile Show—set up in the gym," I tell him. "All kinds of snakes and lizards."

"The Reptile Show? What do they do, little song-and-dance numbers?"

Mom laughs. Her dark red hair is still flat on one side where she slept on it. "Song-and-slither numbers," she says. She reaches over and tucks my shirt label inside. "Go on, honey," she tells me.

"Anyway, they had this yellow python that was as thick as your arm, Dad. But it was too cold in the room, so it didn't do much except blink. They like it warm because they're cold-blooded. And there was this lizard—"

"Calm down, honey," Mom says. "Take a breath. What's the rush?"

They say I talk too fast sometimes, but Dad's always interrupting me, so I have to hurry to get everything in.

"No rush," I say, taking a mouthful of cereal to make Mom happy. "So there was this lizard. It's called a chameleon. It ate three live crickets—they must have starved it or something to eat them on command. It has this tongue that's all sticky with—"

"Hey," Dad says. "I'm trying to eat here. No lizard tongues, okay?"

"You know some people eat cow tongues? Like in sandwiches?"

Dad points a forkful of eggs at me. "What did I just say about tongues?"

Dad interrupting me made me lose my thought. It was a big one too. I tap the spoon against my forehead. "Where was I?"

Mom reaches over and uses her thumb to wipe milk off my forehead. "You were talking about the lizard."

"The chameleon. So Larry got to hold it, and in just seconds it started changing colors. It started off brown and went bright green in like a minute. Green like a new leaf."

"Which one is Larry?" Dad asks.

"Larry Ramirez. Hairy Larry. Remember he came to my birthday party?"

Dad frowns in concentration. "He's the one with the wild hair, sticks straight out?"

"Yeah, it grows that way."

Larry's always getting in trouble for his hair, because it stands out. It's like at the science center, where they have that electric ball you put your hand on and your hair sticks up. Well, he's like that all the time. And when you get Toothpick or Blob looking around for somebody to smack, you don't want to stand out. Like Larry. Like me.

"Chameleons change color because the temperature changes, like when Larry was holding it. Or when they're afraid, so they can camouflage and hide."

Dad finds a ketchup splat on his pocket. He tries to rub it off.

"I think your father's changing colors too. The hard way," Mom says.

I tap my spoon against the tip of my nose. "I was thinking how that would be the most perfect thing."

"What would?" Mom says.

"Like the chameleon," I tell them. "If I could just change colors when I need to. I mean, then there would be no problems."

"Why do you need to change colors?" Dad asks me. "Are you planning some combat missions or something?"

"No. It's just that if you're the right color, you fit in. But the right color keeps changing, so it's better if you can change too. One day you're brown, one day you're green."

Dad looks confused. "My son wants to be a lizard." He turns to Mom. "Where did we go wrong? It must be all those crickets you fed him in the crib."

Dad's always joking. I'm serious. Kind of, anyway. I mean, it's not possible to change colors, but if it was, everything would be perfect. Like the lizard, I could disappear in the leaves, camouflaged. Except the leaves would be the kids at school, and the lizard would be me.

Four

A sick Chihuahua is lying on its back in my lap, looking up at me with shiny black bugged-out eyes. I'm feeding him this special fattening formula for midget dogs from an eyedropper. His name is Titanic.

The owners said he was lost for a week, picked up some worms in his belly and feels totally wiped out. Titanic shivers a bit in my lap but I don't know if he's scared or cold. So I talk to him. "You're a good little shrimp," I say, and tuck the towel protecting my pants around him so he's covered better.

Since I've been best friends with Lynda, her mother has been letting us help out with small stuff on the weekends (small stuff like Titanic here), when the veterinarian's office is closed but the animals still need petting, Milk-Bones and a hand to lick.

Dr. Brook, Lynda's mom, kept a real close eye on me at first. I guess she thought I was going to try and dribble a hamster like a basketball, or put the rabbit suffering from ear mites in with the pit bull.

Dad made me promise to wear gloves at all times, when scooping and around the sick dogs. For a while he wanted me to wear one of those white surgery masks over my nose and mouth when I worked at the vet's. But Mom told him he was being crazy and talked him out of it.

Titanic sneezes three times, fast and wet. He tosses around in my lap until he's tangled in the towel, then shuts his buggy eyes and falls asleep. I put him back in his cage and wash the sneezes off my hands at the sink. Dr. Brook pokes her head into the back room.

"How's the feeding going?" she asks.

I show her the nearly empty container. "Titanic was a real hog. He's sleeping now, but he sneezed three times and he's kind of shivery."

"I'll check his temperature. Want to help? Just grab one of the thermometers from the glass jar there."

Dr. Brook shows me how you take a dog's temp. It ain't pretty. The thermometer doesn't go in his mouth, or his ear, nose or underarm, or between his toes. It goes where (like Dad sometimes says) the sun don't shine.

Titanic's used to this, though. He just opens one eye and makes a sleep-lazy growl.

"No fever," the doctor says. "And sometimes dogs sneeze when they're happy. Try sneezing back at them. It's kind of like shaking hands."

Dogs have this whole language where half of their words are smells and a sniff is a conversation.

"I changed shirts," Lynda says, coming in carrying a squeaky-clean wiener dog. A dachshund.

Dr. Brook brushes a splotch of foam out of Lynda's hair. "I think we shampooed the whole room that time. At least now none of us will get fleas."

Now that I've met both her parents, I can see how Lynda got most of her face from her mom. Lynda's like a cup of coffee—it starts out black, then you add cream. She's about half cream, half coffee. She's got straight hair, real thick—the kind of hair that doesn't move in the wind.

"Can I tell him?" Lynda asks her mom.

"I don't know." Dr. Brook squints at me, smiling. "Can he be trusted?"

"Leftovers is going to be in a dog show," Lynda says. "And he's going to win a medal. And they'll put his picture in the newspaper."

"Hold on," Dr. Brook breaks in. "There might be other beagles just as pretty as Leftovers."

"Impossible. How can you say that? I'm going to tell him you said that." Lynda is so excited her head is sort of rocking back and forth like there's music playing.

A show for dogs. Probably hundreds of dogs. Thousands. "When?" I ask. "Where? Can I go? Does he have to do tricks? Or pass a test?"

Dr. Brook laughs. "All he has to do is be the best beagle he can be."

Then it hits me. Leftovers doesn't have a chance.

"He's only got three legs. They'll take off points, won't they, because he walks funny?"

I know what Dad would say right now. "The system is corrupt." And he'd have a speech ready to tell me how to fix it.

"This is a special dog show," Dr. Brook says. "A show for handicapped dogs, dogs with disabilities. They won't hold a missing leg against him. Every mutt there will have something missing. Leftovers just has to be his beautiful three-legged, one-eared self and he can't help but win."

"Let's go home and tell Leftovers," says Lynda.

"Just give me a minute to lock up. Say bye to all the patients."

I peek in Titanic's cage. The Chihuahua is still wrapped in his towel, drooling as always. He sneezes twice in his sleep. He must be happy. So I sneeze back good-bye.

Five

Mom's making pizza when I get home from the vet's. She grates three kinds of cheese to cover up all the vegetables she puts on, so I won't know I'm eating them.

"I fed a Chihuahua today," I tell her. "Fed him this goopy stuff from a bottle, just like he was a baby."

"Is he sick?"

"Yeah, but he's getting better. He just has to put on weight, not too much because they only ever weigh about five pounds, full grown."

I grab some shredded cheddar.

"Did Lynda help?" Mom asks.

I shake my head. "She was busy shampooing a

19

wiener dog, with flea shampoo. She said he was real slippery. You know, they've got a special blow-dryer just for dogs."

I hear Dad come in the front door. A minute later he pokes his head in the kitchen.

"Pizza!" he says. "I was thinking pizza all the way home." He kisses Mom on the back of her neck as she chops the veggies. "You must be psychic."

"I am," Mom tells him. "And reading your mind, I know you're going to try and steal some of my cheese."

She slaps his hand in midair, but he grabs a clump anyway.

"Keath fed a Chihuahua today," she says.

"I got him to eat a whole bottle of his formula. Then he sneezed on me. Because he was happy."

"Better go and wash your hands," Dad says. "You know the rule about pet hair."

How could I forget the rule? It's the law!

I use the kitchen sink and dishwashing liquid to clean up.

"You should use real soap," Dad tells me.

"This is real. It says it kills bacteria. I could probably drink this stuff and never get sick again."

"My son, the biologist!" Dad says. "I don't know if it's a good idea to be spending time around sick dogs."

Mom always says Dad is a neat freak. He likes

everything perfect, neat and tidy. That's his job—security, making sure nothing goes wrong.

Dogs are messy, I know.

If I was a dog I'd be a golden retriever, because I'm blond with brown eyes. Mom would be an Irish setter, because they have red hair like hers. Dad would be a Doberman, or maybe a German shepherd, one of those really alert guard dogs.

"I've never heard of anybody catching a cold from a dog," Mom says. She has to wrestle Dad's hand away from the cheese so she can arrange it on top of the veggies on the dough.

I'm digging in my pocket for the dog show flyer to show him. But maybe I'd better wait till later. A disabled dog show. He might think I'll catch a limp from one of them.

"I was just over visiting your grandmother," Dad says to me.

I've only seen Gran once since she got sick a few months ago. She had a stroke in her brain.

"Is she better yet?"

"Well, she's as better as she's going to get. Strokes are pretty serious. They do a lot of damage to your brain."

"Does she still . . . shake all the time?"

Dad nods. "The doctor says the shaking probably won't go away. But her speech is improving. It's getting easier to understand what she's saying."

When I saw Gran in the hospital, she looked like

a different person. I mean, her face was sort of scrunched up on her left side. The doctor said that whole side of her body was partly paralyzed, so she could hardly move it and had to use a wheel-chair. Her tongue was half frozen too, so she had to learn to speak all over again.

"I'm sure she'd like to see you, Keath," Dad says. "You haven't visited in a while."

"I know. It's just . . ." I don't know how to say it.

"Just what?"

"It's just that she doesn't look like Gran any-more."

I can't look Dad in the eye, because then I'll feel even worse. The truth is, Gran scares me now. The way she looks, it's like she's haunted or something. And she talks funny now, slurring all her words. I miss her and everything, but I can't go see her half destroyed like that.

"She's still Gran," Dad tells me. "She just got sick. She's still the same on the inside."

Mom slides the pizza in the oven and wipes her hands on the dish towel. "When I dropped in on her last week," she says, "she was asking what you were up to. I told her about your dog-walking."

"Oh yeah? What did she say?" I ask.

"She told me she had dalmatians when she was growing up, two of them."

"I didn't know that."

Mom shrugs. "There's lots of things you don't know that only Gran can tell you."

She comes over and fixes my hair. It's parted down the middle but it's always getting messed up, so she makes sure the part is straight. Then she bends down and kisses the top of my head. She smells like cheese melting, or maybe the whole room does. But when she bends down and her long red Irish setter hair surrounds me, the rest of the room disappears and I feel safe. It's impossible to feel bad when she's so close.

Six

Me and Lynda push our chairs together at the table in the school library. We've got a stack of dog books to go through. There's zero information on three-legged dogs. The guides to breeds tell you what makes a perfect poodle or collie. There's nothing in there about totally imperfect beagles.

"Oh no," Lynda says in a low voice. "Don't look up."

So of course I do.

Blob just walked into the library. He looks around, but his eyes don't stop on me. Blob must have been one of those fifty-pound babies you see in the *National Enquirer;* must have been born hungry.

Lucky for us, he's alone. Blob is harmless as long as he's not with Toothpick. Blob is like a pile of oily rags—as long as there's no match to light it on fire, you're safe. But Toothpick burns like a blowtorch. Put the two of them together and you're toast.

We keep our heads down and Blob walks right past us to the science fiction section. We go back to the dog books.

"Hey," Lynda says. "There's Leftovers."

She's pointing to a picture of a beagle sitting back on its hind legs with its two front paws in the air, in the begging position.

"It says here that beagles were hunting dogs originally. For hunting rabbits and quails."

The begging beagle's chest and belly are all white. Some dogs really love belly rubs. Like Leftovers. He squirms on his back and rolls back and forth when you lay him down and rub him there.

"It says they're gentle and loving," Lynda tells me. "Good guard dogs. They love to explore and can wander off. That's Leftovers, totally. That's how he got hurt."

"Did he get lost?" I ask.

"Yeah. He was running around on the loose and got hit by a car. This was before he came to live

with us. His owners brought him to my mom's office—only his name was Predator back then."

I laugh. "Predator? Him?"

"I know. Stupid name. I mean, he's not like a
rottweiler or a pit bull or anything. But anyway, his
owners brought him in with one hind leg crushed
and his left ear torn right off. Mom said his leg
couldn't be saved, the bone was broken in way too
many places. So she had to amputate."

The other day when me and Lynda were on
scooping patrol, we had to wait for a traffic light to
change, and I felt this weight pressing against my
leg. I looked down and there was Leftovers leaning
on me. He can't sit normally like other dogs with
only his one back leg, so he likes to lean on
things—telephone poles, newspaper boxes, hydrants, me. I like it when he leans on me, because
I know he's there even when I'm not looking.

"So what happened?" I ask. "How come he's
living with you now?"

"His old owners, the ones who named him
Predator, didn't want him anymore. They said he
would be too much trouble, they couldn't take
care of him."

I just shake my head. "Leftovers is no trouble.
So he looks a little funny. You can't hold that
against him."

"Yeah," Lynda says. "I mean, you look kind of
funny, but I don't hold it against you."

I give her a couple of fake punches on the shoulder. "I don't look funny."

"Look around, Keath. Hardly anybody else looks like you. Face it, you're vanilla in a chocolate school."

I tap my fingers up the back of her neck, like there's a spider crawling up it. "Oooooooo. It's the attack of the spooky white boy."

Lynda shivers and shakes me off.

"His bite turns you white," I tell her.

She laughs with me. "You're the honky vampire."

"Honk. Honk."

Lynda turns the page and there's a picture of a litter of puppy beagles. I wish I'd known Leftovers when he was tiny like that. I wouldn't have let him get hit by a car. And even if an accident had happened, I'd never have given him up for looking funny.

"When his old owners gave him up, we took him in. And gave him a real name, because without his leg and ear what we had left was Leftovers."

Predator is a crazy name for a beagle. If I had to call anybody Predator, it would be Toothpick. He's got those eyes that can catch any movement a small creature might make. A small creature like me. And just when you think it's safe, he's swooping down on you with his claws out.

I look over at Blob, who's reading a paperback.

He's frowning at the page like any second he might tear the book in two. But he always looks like that. That's his angry face, his happy face, his I-don't-care face. A face like a rock, like a walking Mount Rushmore.

I don't know why Toothpick and Blob hate me so much. But I know if I looked like everybody else, I wouldn't be their main target.

There was this hunting show on TV one time, and the guys in the camouflage suits were saying how the best hunter isn't the one with the best turkey call or the fanciest equipment. The best hunter is the one who sees what sticks out, what doesn't belong, because that's your target.

I go back to the dog books. Dogs don't hate anybody. I want to be a golden retriever when I grow up.

Seven

It's Saturday and I'm at the mall with Mom. I have the day off, from school and scooping. Lynda's dad only does the dog-walking Monday to Friday when people are at work, and Dr. Brook said there was no shampooing or special feedings to do down at the vet's. Titanic went home Wednesday after gaining half a pound.

Mom's looking for a birthday present for Dad.

"What kind of present?" I ask.

Mom studies the map of the mall.

"Don't know," she says. "I'll know what I'm looking for when I find it."

Dad's birthday is in two weeks. The week after that is the dog show. I figure I'll tell Mom first and win her over. Then when I tell Dad, it'll be two against one.

Mom takes forever. I ask if I can just wait in the comics section of the bookstore or meet her later in Pet Palace. But no. Too many news stories on TV about kids getting nabbed from malls. A couple years ago she would have had my hand in her kung fu death grip, but she knows better now.

Mom goes into The Land of Linen, which turns out to be a shop that sells nothing but bedroom stuff, blankets and sheets and junk like that. She walks down the aisle, touching everything—fuzzy cushions and pillows. Dad says Mom thinks with her hands, like those blind people who read books that have popped-up dots instead of printed letters. They read with their fingertips. Mom, too. I leave her alone feeling the flannel blankets.

I turn the corner in The Land of Linen and find the Mountain of Pillows. I think about diving in the middle, but it looks like the mountain would swallow me up and drown me in feathers. There's this one pillow that has a big yellow smiley face on it, with a stick-figure body. For some reason it reminds me of Toothpick. It's those skinny arms and legs. I can imagine sleeping on that pillow and that big smiling mouth opening up at night to eat my head.

I look around before I give it a punch right between those black-dot eyes on its yellow face.

Yeah! Right! In your face, Toothpick!

I give it another shot, this time in the straight
stick of the body. Then I try a combination. Left
jab, left jab and a right to the body.

Still smiling? Oh, you like that? Whitey's got a
little more for you.

I give him a flurry of punches, leaving him no
time to breathe. Lefts and rights flying like hail.

Try to eat my head? Eat this!

"Keath?"

It's Mom. She's standing there with pillowcases
draped over her arm, looking at me like I just swal-
lowed a basketball or something.

"What are you doing?" she asks.

Why is my crazy kid attacking a pillow? she must
be wondering.

I'm breathing hard. Guess I just got lost there
for a second. What do I say?

"Just . . . testing the pillows," I say, shrugging.
I glance away, trying to look bored. "Can we go?"

Mom shakes her head and gives me a funny little
smile that says: You're a raving lunatic, but you're
my raving lunatic.

Out in the mall, beyond The Land of Linen,
Mom finds the perfect gift in Hardware Extra-
ordinaire. They sell fifty kinds of nails and twenty

different hammers. I stop to watch the paint blender, a machine that mixes different colors to get the exact shade the person wants. It shakes the paint can until it's just a blur.

"Keath," Mom calls.

I feel dizzy, like I've been spun around and shaken to a blur. It reminds me how it feels when Toothpick smacks me in the head, and I wish I had that smiley-face pillow so I could give it a knockout punch.

"Over here, Keath."

Mom's standing in front of a safe big enough for me to fit inside. I swing the door open and shut. Pressing my ear to the door, I spin the combination lock and listen to see if I can hear any numbers clicking into place.

"This is great, Mom. I could fit in here," I say, peering inside.

Mom shakes her head. "Which is exactly why we're not getting that one. Besides, we don't have the crown jewels at home. What would we fill it with?"

I'm trying out some combinations on the lock. "We could put the TV in it at night, in case someone broke in and tried to steal it."

Mom smiles and reaches down to fix the part in my hair. "I think you've been watching that paint mixer too long. No, *this* is the one for your father."

She taps the top of a key safe about the size of a computer monitor. No combination or anything, and you probably couldn't even fit our VCR in it.

"I don't know," I say. "Can't someone just break in and carry it off?"

"You bolt it to the floor. Look, it says it's made from titanium, one of the hardest metals in the world." Mom's reading from the brochure. "And it can withstand temperatures exceeding three thousand degrees Fahrenheit."

I knock on the side to see what titanium feels like. "You could dip this thing in molten lava," I say.

"And you never know when a volcano will erupt in New York."

I nod. "We need a safe to be safe."

"Your dad will love this."

I try pounding on the top to see what it sounds like.

"Hey. Hey. Don't scuff it up," Mom says. "You already assaulted a pillow today. God, what are they putting in those school lunches?"

As soon as Mom says the word *lunch,* I'm starving.

"Can we eat?" I ask.

"Okay. But let's go outside. The fresh air will clear out that crazy head of yours."

Mom brushes her hand on my cheek. She can't help it. She's thinking with her fingers.

Mom pays for the safe and hauls it outside, grunting all the way. "I don't think we have to worry about anybody stealing this. They'll get a massive hernia just getting it down the stairs."

We sit on a bench by the old courthouse, me and Mom with the safe between us. It's fall, but the sun's out and I'm holding a jumbo veggie smokie (a hot dog) in my hand, so I'm not cold. Mom's trying to stuff a smokie buried in fried onions into her mouth. It ain't pretty.

"So where's Dad? Working overtime?" I mumble around a mouthful.

Mom swallows. "He went to see Gran. At the retirement home the families usually visit on Saturday, so he didn't want her to feel forgotten."

"Oh."

Forgotten? Is that how she feels? I mean, I haven't seen her in a while—all right, a long while—but that doesn't mean I've forgotten her. It's just that she's so different, I don't know what to say to her anymore.

I pinch off a piece of my bun and toss it to a couple of pigeons. They tear it up between them.

"Do you think she misses me?" I ask.

Mom pokes at a tangle of onions trying to escape her bun. "I know she does. She's always asking about you."

"Is her face still . . . you know, frozen?"

Mom throws a string of onion to the birds. They

give it the eye but don't seem to know what to do with it.

"She's gotten a little better," Mom tells me. "But her left side is still mostly paralyzed. She talks now, but you have to listen closely to get what she's saying."

I toss another chunk of bun and the birds dive for it in a mob. I think that's all they eat in the wild, loaves of bread.

"The other day Gran said to ask if you were still making hoppers. I had to ask her what hoppers were."

I smile. "They're frogs. We used to call them hoppers. Remember when she showed me how to make them out of folding paper?"

"Origami," Mom says. "You used to love that stuff."

"Yeah." The hoppers we made from paper could even do a little jump when you tapped them on the back end. *Hoppers* is like a secret password only me and Gran would know. Just thinking about those frogs makes me miss her.

Mom reaches over to wipe a blob of ketchup off my knee. "You're a big old slob like your mom."

We stuff our faces and watch the birds watching us eat. Mom finishes off her dog and wipes her mouth. A small gray bird lands right by my foot. I toss it a big chunk for being so brave.

I should be so brave, and go and see Gran.

We get up and lift the safe between us, grunting over to the curb. We must look like we just robbed a bank. Okay, a really small bank. And we couldn't crack the safe.

Mom hails a cab and we make our getaway.

Eight

I'm dead. I know it. If I called the Psychic Friends Hotline right now they'd just hang up— no use talking to a dead kid. I know I'm dead because of what I saw this morning.

Dad dropped me off and honked twice like always before he drove away to work. My breath clouded in the air. I looked up at the blue-ice sky and down at my feet making crunching sounds on the frosted grass.

When we walk the dogs after school now, a couple of the terriers have to wear sweaters. They don't seem to mind so much. It's just getting the sweaters over their heads they don't like, so they whimper or growl to tell you to hurry up.

I was thinking about those little sweaters when I looked up from my frost-crunching feet and saw Toothpick and his older brother standing outside the fire door. Toothpick was backed up against the door. His brother, who's about fifteen, real tall and thin, was pointing his finger at Toothpick's forehead.

"Got that! Got that! Got that!" the brother was saying, poking him in the head each time he repeated it.

"Got it." I could barely hear Toothpick's voice. It didn't even sound like him.

"Can't hear you."

"I said I got it."

There was something familiar about the way Toothpick sounded. It reminded me of those times when my eyes tear up and my nose starts to run, and I try to swallow it all down so it won't show. But then my throat closes up, like I could hear Toothpick's was closing right then.

I shouldn't have stared at them standing there by the fire door. Should have just turned my head and gone inside. But I'm an idiot. I stared.

Toothpick saw me staring.

So I know I'm dead now. Because I saw him when I wasn't supposed to.

In class, I try to act like there's nothing wrong, but pretty soon Lynda figures something's up.

"What's wrong?" she asks.

We're in the middle of an experiment with baking soda, a plastic pop bottle and a balloon, wearing our science lab aprons so our clothes won't get all mucked up.

"Nothing." I shrug.

Lynda picks a purple piece of wax off her apron, from when we made candles a couple of weeks ago. The wax has hardened into a perfect round drop, like a teardrop falling from my chin or a blood drop dripping from the tip of my nose. I know I'll be seeing the color of my blood real soon.

"What kind of nothing?" Lynda wants to know.

The balloon attached to the top of the pop bottle is expanding because of the science happening inside.

"The kind of nothing where there's nothing I can do about it. It's going to happen, that's all."

Foam is fizzing inside the bottle like a slow-motion explosion.

"What's going to happen?" Lynda digs her thumbnail into the wax drop, breaking it in two.

"Toothpick's going to beat the crap out of me."

"Why?"

All around us balloons are swelling up, filling with chemistry. Some kids are shaking their bottles to make the balloons go faster.

"I saw his big brother kind of slapping him around."

Lynda picks another drop of wax off her apron and sets it carefully on top of our balloon.

"Well, maybe . . . maybe . . ." But she can't think up a maybe.

I sigh. "No maybes."

Right then our big experiment turns into a big mess. The thing we forgot, even though it's written on the board in neon green chalk, is that we were supposed to hold the balloon on the bottle with an elastic band. We even have the band, except it's around Lynda's wrist where it isn't doing any good.

Fizzy foam and foamy fizz are everywhere, including up my nose. Lynda is blinking some out of her eyes.

But at least we aren't the only idiots. Two other groups are soaked too.

"Not to worry," the teacher says, patting me on the shoulder. "You're the reason they invented aprons."

I look at Lynda looking at me, my nose running with fizz, her face covered in baking-soda drool. It's too much.

Even though I'm dead, I can't help laughing.

Now it's lunch. Today's special is spaghetti. I pass my plate over to Hairy Larry. If you're going to get beat up, it's better to have an empty stomach.

Toothpick's been keeping an eye on me from

the other side of the cafeteria. He's got spaghetti sauce dripping from his chin.

If life was a TV nature special, Toothpick would be a gorging lion feeding on his prey, warm blood dripping from his chin. No, hold it. Toothpick would be a cheetah. Real thin, real fast, real mean. Lynda would be a zebra, white with chocolate-ripple stripes. And me? I'd be a little blond mouse hiding in the tall grass, sniffing the wind for any danger.

Through the grass I see the cheetah. And it sees me. The cheetah licks spaghetti sauce from its lips.

I know what I have to do.

"I'm going outside for a minute," I tell Lynda.

"What? Are you crazy? The second you step out, he's going to get you. In here you're sort of safe, with the crowd. He won't do much with the teachers around."

Larry nods. "Lay low, man. In a couple of weeks he'll forget all about it."

I steal a peek at Toothpick. His eyes are on me.

"It's going to happen sometime. Sooner or later. I can't take him staring at me all the time like this. Got to get it over with."

I can see Lynda is thinking about arguing, but then she just shakes her head. "Do you want me to come with?"

"No," I say.

Better to be squashed in private. He'll throw a

41

punch and I'll go down fast. I'll take a dive and hope that's enough.

"If you're not back in five minutes . . . ," Lynda says.

"Call for a hearse."

I walk down the hall and out the front door into the bright sun. This would be a nice day if it wasn't my funeral. My breath hangs like white smoke in the air.

I'm a blond mouse creeping out of the safe shade of the tall grass.

Behind me the school doors bang open. If this was a nature special, the mouse would run like mad and the cheetah would chase. No contest. The mouse runs but he never gets away. I turn and face Toothpick.

He's alone. No Blob. Usually Toothpick brings him along to watch, like his own personal audience.

"Hey, Whitey," he says. "Whatcha doing out here in the sun? Trying to get a tan?"

Now that he's up close, I can see a small bruise on the left side of his head near his eye. I look down and wait for the punch. My knees are so shaky I won't have to take a dive, I'll just crumple. His elbows look extra pointy today, like he sharpened them last night.

"Man, you're so white you'd glow in the dark."

Toothpick jabs his fingers into my chest.

"Don't be watching me all the time, Mayonnaise," he tells me. "I don't want to catch you watching me."

This is the most he's ever talked to me. I think he wants me to say something. But anything I say will be the wrong thing.

"You got it?" he asks, shoving my shoulder and making me step back.

"Yes," I say in my mouse's voice.

Another shove. "Got it?"

"Yes." I say it louder.

Even though I know it's coming, it's still a shock when his fist hits me in the gut. I fall. On my knees, staring at the ground, I can see his shadow. I see the shadow of his arm rising up again and wait for it to fall on my head. But no. His shadow takes a step back. I stay down, trying to breathe.

"Good," Toothpick says.

There's a second where time freezes and I'm sure he's going to move in and smash me. But then I watch as his shadow moves off. The school doors open and shut.

One shot in the gut? That's all? Maybe his heart wasn't in it. Getting hit by his brother must have done that.

I get up and take a long breath of cold air. I'm still catching my breath when Lynda finds me sitting on the front steps in the sun.

"You alive?" she asks.

I nod.

"Hungry? Look. It's magic," Lynda says, pulling two Twinkies out of her sleeve.

I take one and peel back the wrapper.

"What else you got up there?" I ask.

"Anything you want. How about some spaghetti?" Lynda makes like she's going to pull a big mess of it out of her sleeve.

I laugh. "No thanks." I take a bite of the Twinkie. "How about a curse? You do those?"

"I think he's already got a curse on him."

"What do you mean?" I say.

"His brother."

"Yeah. I guess so." I finish my Twinkie and Lynda hands me the other one.

We sit in the sun, the mouse and the zebra, safe from the cheetah for now.

Nine

On our dog walks after school we always take the same route. Lynda's father says the dogs like it that way, so they can visit the same trees and hydrants every day. They each have their favorites. Mr. Brook waits for us in front of the school and we walk down a few blocks, past the community center to the park. Then we backtrack past the school to Lynda's place.

Mom's working at the center today. She teaches this class for adults called English as a Second Language. It's for people from other countries who speak Chinese, Korean and Russian and stuff. She teaches them the basics.

"Hey, Mr. Brook," I say. "Can I go in and show Leftovers to my mother? She works here."

He's busy keeping the small dogs separated from the big ones, because if you get them mixed up the little guys get shoved around.

"Tell you what," he says. "You go in and I'll take the pack down to the park. Meet you back here in fifteen."

"Can I go too?" Lynda asks.

"Sure. But if these dogs eat me alive, you're going to have to explain it to Mom."

The pack leads Mr. Brook away toward the park, small dogs on the left, big dogs on the right.

On the doors to the community center we discover a No Dogs sign. It shows the silhouette of a dog with a line drawn through it, crossing it out. Leftovers sniffs the door and looks up at us.

"Don't take it personally," I tell him.

"Here," Lynda says. "Unzip your jacket."

"Why?" I ask, unzipping my black windbreaker. "Are we going to dress him up?"

Lynda gives me a look. "Well, that's one idea. But how about you wear the jacket and we stuff him inside and zip it up?"

"You're a genius," I say.

She nods. "That's what they tell me."

We pick Leftovers up and I hug him close while Lynda works on the zipper. It's a tight fit. Leftovers squirms a bit, sticks his head out and noses my chin. But he doesn't seem to mind too much.

"How does it look?" I ask. "Can you tell?"

Lynda steps back to take a look. "It's still pretty obvious. Just make sure his head's stuck in when we pass the desk. And here . . ." She picks up a thin newspaper, one of those free ones you see around, from a pile by the doors. "Open it up and make like you're reading something," she says.

We walk in the center, with me trying to hold Leftovers in and keep the newspaper open at the same time. The beagle shifts around. He doesn't like having his head covered, so he makes a little whining sound just as we're passing the desk.

The man at the desk looks over at us. Lynda fakes a cough.

"Asthma," she tells him, trying to sound hoarse.

He gives us a look but lets us go by.

"Good one," I whisper to her.

"I'm a genius, remember?"

We check out the rooms on the second floor and find Mom finishing up after a class. There's only one student left, a gray-haired man sitting near the front.

"What are the nouns in this sentence?" Mom asks, pointing at the blackboard. The sentence written there reads: "The bus goes over the bridge."

"Okay," the man says. "The now-uns in the sentence are . . . *bus* and . . . *bridge*."

"Perfect," Mom tells him.

I catch Mom's eye, waving from the door.

"Hey, guys, come on in," she says. She pats the front of my windbreaker. "I think you've put on a few pounds since I last saw you. Hi, Lynda."

Leftovers pokes his head out.

"We smuggled him in to meet you," Lynda tells her.

I set him down on the floor and he goes over to inspect Mom.

"So you're the famous three-legged beagle," she says. "I've heard all about you." She scratches under his chin and straightens his fake ear. "Keath, you know Mr. Kim. And Mr. Kim, this is Lynda Brook."

I turn around. The gray-haired student lives across the street from us. He's always wearing this Yankees baseball cap that looks older than Babe Ruth.

"Hi, Mr. Kim," I say. "I thought you already spoke English."

"I can speak pretty good, but I want to read English. I always get the Korean newspaper. Now I want to read the *New York Post*." Mr. Kim reaches back and pulls a folded-up copy of today's newspaper from his jacket pocket.

48

Leftovers tries to hop up on the teacher's chair, but it's too high for him with just the one back leg doing the hopping. Mom lifts him up and sets him in the chair.

"There you go. You can teach the next class for me," she tells him. "How's your grammar?"

Mr. Kim packs up his things, stuffing the *Post* in his bag.

"I'll see you Friday," Mom says to him. "Then we'll start on verbs. Action words."

Mr. Kim nods. "Bye, kids. Bye, dog."

When he's gone, Mom wipes the board clean.

"So how was school today?" she asks. "Any *problems?*"

Lynda gives me a look. We both know Mom means problems of the Toothpick kind.

"Not really," I say, remembering how it felt getting the wind knocked out of me.

Mom gives me a frown. "Not really? Meaning, yes really?"

I shrug. She's always reading my mind.

She reaches over and fixes my hair. I can smell the soap she uses, like apples.

"We'll talk later," she tells me.

"Okay."

Lately Dad and Mom have been talking about maybe moving me to another school. But then there would be no Lynda, no Hairy Larry, no dog walks after school. I've kind of been hoping Tooth-pick would just blow over, but he's like a tornado that never stops.

Leftovers tries to get up on the desk. He's always the explorer. Mom sets him down on the floor before he can mess up her papers.

"We should go," I say. "Mr. Brook will be waiting for us out front with the rest of the pack."

Mom and Lynda help me zip Leftovers back in place to smuggle him out. I look down at the bulge in my jacket and the beagle head sticking out.

"Can you tell?" I ask them.

Lynda nods. "We'll have to use the newspaper again."

"Keep an eye on him, Lynda," Mom says.

"Which one? Keath or Leftovers?"

"Both." Mom smiles. "See you at home," she says, kissing my cheek.

While she's bent close, Leftovers gives her chin a lick.

"Kisses to you, too," Mom tells him.

Ten

"What is this?" Mom says, holding up a thick clump of red-brown hair. She picked it off the sleeve of Dad's coat.

Dad just got home from visiting Gran. He looks at the clump. "That's dog hair."

"Dog hair!" me and Mom say at the exact same time. We're in shock.

"I know," Dad says. "The hairy beast wouldn't leave me alone." He goes over to the kitchen sink and starts washing his hands. "They have this program over at the retirement home where they bring in pets to visit and brighten the place up. Seems to work. Some of those old guys just stare into space most of the day, but when they get a cat in their lap they start petting and talking to it."

Mom tries to throw the ball of hair in the garbage, but I grab it and hold it up to the light.

"What kind of dog was it?" I ask.

"I don't know. One of those big dogs, the ones that live up in the mountains. What are they?"

I try to think. "Um. A husky?"

"No."

"A chow chow?" They're those big orange lion-dogs that have black tongues.

"No."

What else is there? A mountain dog. Big. The clump is mostly reddish brown with some black mixed in.

"A Saint Bernard?"

"That's it. One of those. A big thing," Dad tells me. "It breathed all over me."

"I've never met a Saint Bernard," I say.

Over on the refrigerator door I keep a list of all the kinds of dogs I've met. I check it. There's no Saint Bernard. So I run upstairs and get my guide to dog breeds. I almost kill myself coming back down the stairs at full speed, reading the Saint Bernard listing at the same time.

"Listen to this," I tell them.

Dad groans. "Oh, God. Not the dog book again."

I've been torturing Mom and Dad, reading them pages and pages about pooches. Now when I bring the book out they try to escape.

"You said I could read you one page a day. Didn't he, Mom?"

Mom nods. She never minds when I try and sneak in an extra couple of pages. She pretends she doesn't notice.

"Has he read any pages already today?" Dad asks Mom.

Mom shakes her head, even though after breakfast I did sort of show her pictures of all the different kinds of dachshunds there are (everybody calls them wiener dogs because they have long sausage-like bodies).

"Okay." Dad gives in. "Let's hear it."

First I show the picture to them and make sure this was the dog Dad met.

"That's him. Big slobbering thing," Dad says.

So I read a page out loud. Well, it's actually two pages. I can't just stop in the middle.

Saint Bernards come from the Swiss mountains, where there's a monastery called Saint Bernard's. The monks there train the dogs to rescue people lost in the mountains. The dogs work in teams of three, so when they find somebody, two of them lie down beside him to keep him warm while the third runs for help.

They can weigh up to a hundred and seventy

pounds. One picture shows a kid riding one like a horse, they're that big.

"They have such sad faces," Mom says.

"Yeah. Their faces are kind of droopy. But they can't help that. Even when they're happy they look that way. So, Dad, what did the dog do? Did you pet it?"

Dad makes a face. "What, are you crazy?"

I can only shake my head. Dad just doesn't get it.

"No," he says. "It made the rounds. You know, sticking its head in people's laps, getting scratched and petted. Oh yeah, and it ate four cupcakes before anybody could stop it. Those things are like food vacuums, sucking up everything in their path."

"Just like you," Mom tells me. "I think you must be part dog, from your father's side of the family, of course." She scratches me behind the ear like I'm a hound, so I let my tongue hang out and pant.

"I'm living in the nuthouse," Dad says. "Nuts all over the place."

We all laugh. Us nuts like to laugh.

"Did Gran meet the Saint Bernard?" I ask.

"Actually, there was this wiener dog she liked best. She's still in the wheelchair most of the time, and this little dog got up on the footrest and tried to climb her leg."

"I read how it's bad for their backs," I tell Dad. "With those really long short dogs, it hurts their backs to jump up on things. Even jumping up on couches is bad for them. Dr. Brook says you have to make ramps for them, or some kind of stairs, so they can get up on chairs and things."

Dad nods. "Gran wanted to hold it, so I lifted it up into her lap."

"What about the Saint Bernard?"

"It licked an old guy's face and left candy sprinkles from the cupcakes on his cheek." Dad shakes his head.

I look at the photo in the book. That sad droopy face. Those long flappy ears and big brown eyes.

I *have* to meet this Saint Bernard! And I *have* to go see Gran, before she thinks I've forgotten her totally. With all the dogs there, I can be brave enough to see her, even if she isn't the same anymore. I take the clump of dog hair and stick it between the pages of the dog guide like a bookmark.

"Can I go see Gran next time, when the Bernard's going to be there?" I ask.

Mom and Dad both look surprised.

"Gran would love that," Dad says.

Right then it hits me that I should ask for something. I mean, since I just did a good thing, Dad will let me have one wish. That's the way he works. He's like one of those magic genies—only a cheap one. You only get one wish out of him instead of three. And I know what I want.

"Wait right here, okay?" I tell them. "Don't move."

I run up to my room and grab the flyer for the dog show where Leftovers is going to compete. It's stuck on a spine of the cactus in the corner of my room.

I race back down and show them the flyer.

"You have to read this!" I say. "It's going to be the greatest show. Only special dogs are allowed. Like Leftovers."

"The one with three legs?" Mom asks.

"That's him. He's probably going to win a medal. But there'll be all kinds of breeds and categories and everything. And Lynda's mom will be with us. I have to go. It'll be the greatest show ever."

Dad looks up from the flyer, and I know he's giving in. "Okay," he says.

This is the best. I get to go to the show and meet a Saint Bernard. And see Gran again.

Eleven

I'm looking at one of the top ten saddest things, right up there with Bambi's mom getting killed and that spider in *Charlotte's Web* going to sleep forever.

This sad thing is Titanic, the sick Chihuahua, with half his head shaved. He's back in the vet's with bad ear mites. Dr. Brook had to shave him to get rid of the "infestation."

Under his gray hair, Titanic has pale pink skin. It feels so soft, like suede. Dr. Brook finishes cleaning out his ears with cotton balls, and now Titanic starts smacking his lips. In Chihuahua-speak that means "Put food in here! Now!"

So I do. He's back on his fattening formula for

dwarf dogs. He could use some fat to stop him from shivering so much.

At the next table, Lynda is combing the tangles out of a long-haired Himalayan's fur. It's one of those cats that can't live in the real world because it needs someone to take care of it. Himalayans have little pushed-in noses, so they have trouble breathing sometimes.

A giant white fur ball floats through the air and lands beside Titanic. He eyes it in case it might attack and gives it a weak swat, hitting it off the table and into the air. Titanic's so tired he's not even interested in the cat.

"So how do they grade the dogs at the show?" I ask.

"There's all these different areas they mark them on. Like obedience. Obeying commands."

"Leftovers doesn't do that great with commands, does he?"

"No. But that's because he's got his own brain. He's not a robot."

Titanic bats my hand. I'm not holding his bottle high enough. "Okay, okay," I tell him, lifting it up. I'm good at obeying commands. Maybe I should enter a show.

"And then there's posture. Or they call it poise. How he stands, you know. If he slouches or doesn't stay straight."

"But they don't take points off for standing on three legs?" I say.

"No. As long as he postures himself the best he can. They even have two-legged dogs, with wagons to help them walk."

"Get out."

"It's true. Ask my mom. They have special wagons made for them. Most of the ones I've seen lost their two back legs, so they sit in their wagons and scoot around pretty fast."

"What else?" I ask.

"Let's see. They judge on how the dog moves, walks and runs. They check his coat, make sure it's nice and shiny."

"We'll have to brush and polish him, right?"

"Yep. He's got his own brush at home."

Lynda finishes getting the Himalayan all smooth and untangled. It's way too pretty, and it watches poor Titanic as if he's a scummy butt sniffer. And he is, but in a great way.

"How are we doing in here?" Dr. Brook walks in, peeling off a pair of rubber gloves.

She uses a tissue to wipe the fur around the Himalayan's eyes clean. Cats don't cry, but their eyes leak sometimes if they catch a draft or get dust in them. Lynda's mom pets the cat, running her fingers through the puffball's fur, checking for knots.

"Perfect," she says. "Are we beautiful?" she asks the cat.

It blinks its pool-water blue eyes at us. It knows it's beautiful. It's easy to be when you're born that way, doesn't mean anything.

But Titanic here is beautiful too, because he's a survivor. It's not easy to be a dwarf dog with buggy eyes and a half-shaved head and still be beautiful. Titanic's got everything going against him, so it means more than the beauty of old pool blue eyes over there with its snowy minky fur.

"What else do they judge Leftovers on, Mom? So far we've got posture, obeying, standing and walking good. And having a shiny coat."

"They also look at how healthy the dog is, whether it's alert and clear-eyed. If it's good-tempered. Personality."

"Leftovers is going to score big there," I say. "He's so friendly. Do they take points off if he sniffs the judge's crotch or anything?"

Dr. Brook smiles and shakes her head. "I think they let that pass."

Titanic finishes his bottle and starts blowing milky bubbles, smacking his lips, smiling a doggy smile.

"How's this Chihuahua doing, anyway? Is he getting better?" I say.

Dr. Brook flips through her patient charts. "He's gained half a pound on the new formula.

That's excellent. The adults only weigh four or five pounds. They're the smallest dogs in the world. He's clean and debugged. He'll be going home on Monday."

"He looks pretty funny," I say.

She shines her pocket flashlight into his ears. They look all clean.

"The fur will grow back. He'll have a new, soft gray coat to show off to the girl Chihuahuas."

Lynda puts the Himalayan back in its cage. It curls up in the back and tucks its head in so its forehead is pressing on the floor of the cage. Sleep time.

Dr. Brook closes everything up and dims the lights in back so the animals will know it's night.

In the car, before they drop me off, I tell them I won't be able to scoop after school on Wednesday.

"Where you going?" Lynda asks.

"I'm going to see my grandmother. She lives in an old people's home, since she had a stroke in her brain. They have cats and dogs that visit there twice a week."

"Therapy pets," Lynda's mom says. "They really help sick and mentally handicapped people reach out."

"There's going to be a Saint Bernard visiting the home."

"Now, those are big dogs. The adults run from one-fifty to a hundred and seventy pounds."

Lynda turns to look at me in the backseat. "What's she like?"

"I haven't met it yet. It'll be my first Saint Bernard."

She shakes her head. "Not the dog. Your grandmother."

"She used to be great. She's pretty smart, helped me make some airplane models and stuff. But since she had a stroke, she's . . . you know, kind of *different.*"

I sort of want to say *strange* or *creepy,* but I don't want to be betraying Gran or anything. Even if it's the truth.

Twelve

Dad gets off early Wednesday and picks me up after school. I wave to Lynda, who's off to walk the dog pack with her father. I almost wish I was going with her.

"Remember that movie *Cujo?*" Dad asks as he pulls away from the curb.

"*Cujo?*"

"That Stephen King movie with the killer dog."

"Oh. Yeah. That was a stupid movie," I say.

"Wasn't Cujo a Saint Bernard?"

I try and think. "Yeah. I guess he was."

Dad's still wearing half his uniform, without the jacket and walkie-talkie. He's wearing his favorite tie, which has a blue paisley pattern. *Paisley* means these squiggly tadpole-shaped things that look like they've been swimming around on his tie.

"That wasn't a real dog," I say. "He was an actor."

"An actor?" Dad laughs.

"Cujo is made up. A Saint Bernard wouldn't really do that. And besides, Stephen King isn't real. He's made up too."

"I don't know about that last part," Dad says when we stop, waiting for a light to change. He looks over at me, smiling. So I know he was just fooling with me. He knows Cujo isn't real. Maybe Stephen King is, but I doubt it.

Even though he made me mad, I can't help smiling back. Just when I think Dad is the most dead serious guy in the universe, he pulls one of his jokes.

The light changes and we drive ahead.

"So how's school?" Dad asks.

I shrug. "I don't know."

"Don't know? That sounds mighty suspicious."

Dad's always a guard, even when he's off duty. He notices things.

"School's okay," I say. "It's just I'm practically the only white kid there. I'm like a freak."

Dad frowns. "That kid still bugging you? The one who was pushing you around?"

"Sometimes. I try and stay out of his way."

"You let me know if he starts roughing you up

again," Dad says. He looks over at me with his Doberman watchdog eyes. They don't miss a thing.

"You've made some friends there, though. Lynda and that kid with all the hair . . ."

"Hairy Larry."

"Right, Larry. Frederick Douglass is a pretty good school. You know I went there when I was a kid."

I shrug. "I guess it's okay."

"I grew up in this neighborhood," Dad says. "It can be a tough place sometimes. But we have good neighbors."

"I guess," I say. "But there's no kids on our block. It's all old people."

"It's changed from when I was a kid. You know, our house used to be my uncle Jim's."

I nod. "Before he moved to Florida."

Dad smiles. "I've always loved that house. When I was a kid, Uncle Jim used to have this giant wrench he kept in the closet. I found it in there one day and dragged it out to ask what it was for. He said it was a secret, said it was a special kind of wrench you couldn't buy in stores. But he wouldn't tell me the secret."

Dad stops at a red light and looks over at me. "So, a few months later we were visiting. This was in the dead heat of August. We were sitting there eating Creamsicles, watching a Yankees game on

TV. And Uncle Jim turns to me. 'It's time you learned the secret of the giant wrench.' He went to the closet and pulled it out. I followed him out and down the stairs to the curb. The street was deserted. It was too hot to breathe outside. Uncle Jim lifted the wrench up above his head and said, 'Behold the secret!' Then he went up to the fire hydrant, set the wrench in place and yanked down on it. The hydrant opened up, and it was like a geyser blasting out cold water down the street. Kids came out of nowhere, screaming. Uncle Jim stuck his head in the stream and hollered. 'Sometimes the water's so cold you *have* to shout,' he said."

The light turns green and we drive on.

"Where did he get the wrench?" I ask.

"Years back, he used to be a volunteer fireman in upstate New York. He kept the wrench as a souvenir."

"What happened to it?"

"Must be in the basement somewhere. There's not much call to crack open the hydrant anymore. No kids around to enjoy it."

Sounds like things were way more fun on our block when Dad was a kid.

"Yeah, the neighborhood's changed," says Dad. "But we couldn't afford a nice house like ours anywhere else. And it's close to where Gran is now.

There are other schools, though. Franklin Elementary is only a few blocks further on.''

"Don't know anybody at Franklin," I say.

"It's something to think about." Dad shrugs. "And you're not a freak. Don't call yourself that. There's no such things as freaks, only different kinds of people."

"What about those guys in the circus who eat glass and hammer nails up their noses?" I ask. "Aren't they freaks?"

Dad laughs. "But that's their job. Their career."

He pulls over to the curb. "This is it."

"This place?" I say.

When Dad said nursing home, I was thinking of a big old house with grandmothers and grandfathers sitting on a porch. Maybe some trees with people in wheelchairs under them. But this is a new building on a big street. No old folks in sight. I guess they don't air them out too much.

"Ready?" Dad asks.

"I guess."

There's going to be a dog inside, I tell myself. A big dog. One I've never seen before. A Saint Bernard to add to the checklist.

If there's going to be a hundred-and-fifty-pound dog in the room with me and Gran, I'll be all right.

I flick the lock on the door and step out.

Thirteen

Inside, the place is as clean as a hospital. No germs here. Dad signs the check-in book and they let us in.

It's so quiet, our footsteps make the only noise. "Gran's up on the third floor," Dad tells me.

He made me wear a long-sleeved shirt, buttoned right up to my neck so it's strangling me, and a clip-on tie. The tie is gray and paisley-patterned like Dad's. I guess if we get separated they'll know we belong together.

We get off the elevator at Three. There's more action on this floor. People are walking up and down the halls, most of them wearing slippers. I feel like I just walked into someone's house and they're getting ready for bed.

I follow Dad to Room 319. He pokes his head in, but there's nobody there.

"Let's try down the hall. There's a recreation room."

I hear the room before I see it. The TV is on way too loud, playing an old movie from one of those channels that only does black-and-white stuff. There are a few old guys sitting on the couch in front of it.

I peek inside and see some tables set up where people are playing card games. There's even a miniature pool table where everything is half-size and the billiard balls look more like Ping-Pong balls.

All the eyes in the room focus on us for a second.

"There's Gran," Dad says. "Over by the window."

Dad walks in. I stay in the doorway a few seconds longer, taking a deep breath before I head inside.

She's sitting in a normal chair, not a wheelchair, holding a thin book up to her face so she can see it better. She circles something on one of the pages with a pen. Dad comes up beside her and puts his hand on her shoulder.

Looking up, she says, "There's my boy." She

slurs the words a bit, but I can still make them out. "My Donny."

Donald is Dad's first name.

"Look who's come with me," Dad says.

I walk around from behind Dad to stand in front of her. I'm staring at the floor, but I force myself to look up. Gran gives me a big smile on the right half of her face. The other half stays frozen.

"Come closer," she tells me. "Let me get a good look at you."

I take another step and she leans forward, squinting at me through her glasses. I kiss her on her good cheek. The frozen half is still kind of crunched up, making her look like she's in pain even though she's okay now. Her eyes are a gray shade of blue, paler than I remember, as if some of the color has drained out of them.

Gran pulls me into a one-armed hug. She gives me half a kiss, as good as she can manage.

"I've missed you, Keath. We've lost so much time."

She takes my hand with her steady hand. It feels nice and cool.

The way she speaks, it's like she's got a cube of Jell-O stuck in her mouth and she's trying to talk around it.

"Did you finish the Junkers?" she asks.

I'm surprised she remembers. The Junkers was

the last model we worked on together. It's one of those German planes from World War II.

"I finished that months ago," I tell her. "Turned out pretty good. I painted it with camouflage colors, three different kinds of green."

I can't believe she remembers it. I thought the stroke would make her forget everything.

"I'd like to see it sometime," she says.

"Sure. I could bring it over." I try and look just at the good side of her face, but it's hard.

"Your tie is on crooked," she tells me. She uses her good hand to reach out and straighten it. "Perfect."

Gran sits back in her chair. Her left hand lies in her lap, shaking a little all the time. It doesn't seem to bother her, but it bugs me. It's like the left half of her body doesn't take orders from her brain anymore. It's scary to see, but it must be even scarier for her, seeing it from the inside.

"Looks pretty awful, doesn't it?" she asks.

"What?"

"This," she says, waving at the bad side of her face.

"No. No. It's not so bad," I tell her.

She gives me a small smile. "Thanks for lying. I can walk a little bit now, with my walker." She points to the metal walker beside her chair. "It helps keep me balanced. I can get from my room to here and back now, as long as I rest in between

71

trips. I have to take baby steps. Takes a while, but I get there."

Dad lifts the walker. "It's pretty light," he says.

Gran nods. "It better be. I'm no weight lifter."

That makes me laugh. She laughs too. Gran used to have a laugh that could rattle the windows and knock furniture over (that's how Dad describes it). Now her laugh is quieter. But it's still good to hear.

Suddenly the volume on the TV goes down.

"We have special visitors," a voice calls from the doorway.

The dogs are here! A terrier, a retriever, a wiener dog—and there! A huge Saint Bernard. A woman takes them off their leashes and they walk toward the crowd in front of the TV. Hands reach out to pet and scratch them.

I look back at Dad with a question on my face.

Dad smiles. "Go ahead. But remember, no face licking."

"I'm just going to say hi to the dogs. Okay, Gran?"

"Sure," she says. "Go for it."

The terrier is already up on the couch, stepping from lap to lap, loving the attention. The old people must have been saving treats for the dogs, because wherever the dogs stick their noses there's a munchie waiting for them. They're not real dog treats—one guy is feeding them peanut butter cookies—but the dogs don't mind.

"Go on, Cheryl," the woman with the leashes tells her Saint Bernard. "Go get pets."

There's a shiny string of drool hanging from her face—the Saint Bernard's face, not the woman's. The big dog hangs back, kind of shy, I guess. She's beautiful. Big chocolate eyes, long flappy ears. Her coat is a pattern of red brown and white. I watch her tail. It's not moving. She must be nervous. Too many people, maybe.

But then her head turns and she looks at me. Her tail twitches and starts a slow wag. We meet in the middle of the room.

Cheryl nudges me in the chest and gives my hand a full-tongue lick. I hope Dad's not watching.

"You're beautiful," I tell her. "You're the best."

Her muzzle has a natural droop to it—Saint Bernards always look sad. Her lips sag and sway when she looks around. She snorts when I scratch her under the chin. Must feel good.

Making sure Dad's not looking—he's talking to Gran with his back to me—I kneel down and hug Cheryl's neck, which is bigger than my waist! She smells like an old carpet left out in the rain.

Lynda's dad had to teach me how to pet big dogs. Because they have thick coats, with huge bones and muscles, you practically have to slap their backs and sides for them to feel it. I do that and watch Cheryl's tail swish faster. It's like a thermometer for how she's feeling. Right now, she's got happy-tail fever.

Over by the couch, an old lady is singing to the retriever, who howls along with her. The terrier's still walking across all the laps on its munchie quest.

I feel a tug on my shirt and look down. Cheryl's got half of my tie in her mouth.

"No. No. You don't want to eat that," I tell her.

But I guess she does. She sucks it up. Like a string of spaghetti. One last tug and the tie comes apart. All that's left around my neck is the clip-on knot; the rest is in her mouth. Quickly I pull her drooping lips apart, but it's too late. A last scrap of gray paisley disappears past that shovel-size tongue.

That is the most amazing thing I've ever seen! She ate my tie! I mean, out walking the dogs with Lynda and her dad, I've seen the dogs eat all kinds of junk they find on the sidewalk. Old potato chip bags, squashed M&M's, pizza crusts, chicken bones. A rottweiler tried to eat a dead pigeon one time, but Lynda's dad fished it out before the dog could swallow.

But a tie! What taste could it have? Or smell, or anything? Don't dogs have any taste buds at all?

Does polyester have some nutrients or vitamins I don't know about?

"I hope that goes down okay," I say to Cheryl. I'm glad she didn't swallow the knot. It might get stuck somewhere.

"Keath," Dad calls.

I grab ahold of Cheryl's collar and bring her over to Gran's chair.

"This is Cheryl. She's a Saint Bernard."

Dad takes a couple of steps back. The dog sniffs the book in Gran's lap. Before I can stop her, Cheryl licks a page and starts chewing.

"Don't eat the book," I tell her. "Don't eat."

Cheryl stops for a second, giving me time to pull the page out of her mouth.

"Sorry, Gran," I say, trying to flatten the page out. It's pretty wet, though.

Gran laughs her quiet laugh. "That's okay. It's just a book of word-find puzzles. The doctor says those puzzles are good exercise for my brain. I've never tried chewing them before."

Gran sets her book on the window ledge. "Big dog. Big sad dog," she says to Cheryl as she rubs the Saint Bernard between the ears.

"She's not really sad," I tell Gran. "They always look like that. You can't really tell by looking at their face how they're feeling. Look at her tail move, that's how she smiles."

"Big fur ball," Gran says. "You're just like me. Your face doesn't tell the real story of how you're feeling."

Pretty soon Gran gets tired, so we walk with her back to her room. It takes forever to make it down the hall, but she says it's good to be on her feet again. She's got a bad limp, seeing how her left leg is mostly frozen. Cheryl follows us halfway, then wanders back to the recreation room.

Before she lies down for a nap, Gran gives me a one-armed hug.

"Bring the Junkers next time," she says.

"I will."

I sneak back down the hall to say bye to Cheryl. I kneel down and give her a big hug. "Bye, Cheryl. I'll see you again. Promise." I kiss her on the top of her head.

"Hey, none of that," Dad tells me.

"You said no face licking. You didn't say I couldn't lick her."

Dad frowns.

"That's a joke, Dad."

Out in the car, strapping on my seat belt, I find some Saint Bernard hair stuck to my shirt, orangey brown.

I gather it up and stick it in my pocket.

"What happened to your tie?" Dad asks, just noticing it now.

I look down like I'm surprised and pull loose the knot that's still hanging from my collar.

"It must have fallen apart somewhere," I say.

I can't tell him. He might not let me see Cheryl again.

I wonder if she'll miss me.

Fourteen

*E*arlier today, when we were walking the dogs in the park, I was thinking the one good thing about Leftovers only having three legs is that he never has to lift his back leg when he pees. Saves a lot of time over the years—time better spent sniffing. Lynda's dad said Leftovers' lost leg is waiting for him in Heaven, hopping in place, killing time until the reunion.

It's one week until the dog show. Lynda's dad made a new leather earflap for the beagle. The old one was looking a little sad, because whenever it falls off Leftovers chews it a bit.

We've trained him to do everything. Well, he already knew how to walk and stand. But now he keeps his head up and alert instead of bent down sniffing the ground. You can't get much training in when you're walking nine dogs. So tonight at Lynda's place, we're teaching Leftovers without all the traffic noise and other dogs to distract him.

You have to bribe dogs to get them to do anything.

What will you give me for sitting? Leftovers asks with his eyes. What do I get for standing still? For rolling over? For lying down?

The answer is usually a Milk-Bone or a peanut-butter-crunch biscuit—they're his favorite. But sometimes he'll settle for belly rubs, or Green Goobers, which is his best-loved squeaky toy (it glows in the dark and gives off a spooky whistle when he bites into it).

Up in Lynda's room, we sit on her bed with Leftovers between us squeaking his Goobers.

"Do you suppose he thinks that thing's alive?" I ask. "I mean, he keeps chewing on it and it keeps making noises."

"I don't know." Lynda sounds doubtful. She's peering in the beagle's ear with one of those special ear flashlights doctors use. "I don't see much going on in there. Here, take a look."

She hands the light over. I lift his ear and squint into the darkness inside his skull.

"Everything's pink in there. I don't see any brain, though."

Lynda laughs. "I think you'd need a microscope for that. Isn't that right, Leftovers?"

He squeaks his toy in answer.

"Can I be there for his bath before show day? Help shampoo him?"

"Sure. It gets pretty wild, so you have to watch out. Dad says he's more slippery than a greased pig when he's lathered up. Leftovers always tries to escape, so you have to hold him firm and cut him off if he's looking to jump out of the tub."

Lynda's got one hand pressed to his side, feeling him breathe. I think she's going to be a vet too someday. I just want to be a dog walker.

"You were pretty mad at school today," I say. "I thought you were going to kill Blob."

"He's such an idiot. Calling me Two-Face. That's all I need is another name for them to call me."

Blob started calling her that after that villain in Batman, the guy who looks normal on one side of his face and crazy on the other.

"You looked like you were going to explode," I say. "He was in shock there when you were yelling at him."

I use the flashlight to look up the beagle's nose. He's one clean hound.

"Some kids look at me and say that I'm black, then some say I'm more white than black, or not black enough. It's stupid. Maybe I'm just Lynda, you know?"

She tugs at Green Goobers, but Leftovers isn't ready to give it up. It lets out a whistley kind of moan, like a boat out at sea.

"Two-Face," she says. "What's that supposed to mean? So which half of me is supposed to be normal and which one's crazy?"

"I don't think Blob thought about it real hard."

I check out Leftovers' teeth with the light. He keeps an eye on me. I guess I'm getting too close to his beloved Goobers.

"You know Ronnie, that rottweiler my dad walks? I should bring him to school one day and just lock him up with Toothpick and Blob in a closet or something."

"*Those* are real angry dogs. Bad tempers."

"Yeah," Lynda says. "But I bet they'd find out they were all related, or they all eat raw meat for lunch."

"Yeah."

"What do you say, Leftovers?"

He squeaks his toy.

Lynda shakes her head. "That's your answer for everything."

Fifteen

Mom says it's supposed to be a big surprise. She rushed home after her class at the community center to get everything set up. We're going to wait in the kitchen in the dark when Dad comes home. So, to make it a really big surprise, I run out to the garage and get Dad's air horn from his toolbox. It's small, about the size of Dr. Brook's ear flashlight. I guess it honks or something. It's for emergencies.

Mom lights the candles on Dad's cake when we hear him pull up outside. Then she stands in the shadows by the light switch. I crouch over by the stove.

"I'm home!" Dad calls from the hallway.

We stay quiet. I swallow a giggle fit and hold out the air horn, with my thumb ready to press down.

"I'm home!" He's closer, just outside the kitchen door.

The door swings open. Mom hits the lights. We both shout, "Surprise!"

But you can't hear us, because right then I hit the button on the horn and blast the whole house. It's the loudest noise I've ever heard. I'm surprised the cake candles aren't blown out and fridge magnets aren't scattered on the floor.

I don't know who looks more scared. Dad throws up his hands. Mom screams. I drop the horn on the floor as if it stung me. We all just stand there gasping for a minute. Dad's face looks really white—I mean whiter than white.

Then he sees the cake and starts shaking his head and laughing in a shocked kind of way.

"Are you trying to kill me?"

"Surprise," Mom says, taking his hand and patting it.

"Right," he says. "Surprise. I'm very surprised."

When he catches his breath, Mom gets him to blow out his candles.

"Did you make a wish?" she asks.

"Yeah. I wished I never bought that stupid air horn."

They start laughing, and I join in when I see I'm not in big trouble.

Mom cuts the first slice of the quadruple chocolate cake and gives it to Dad.

"Happy birthday," she tells him.

He holds a hand up to his ear like he can't hear. "What's that?"

"Happy birthday!" we shout together at him.

We don't actually have to fake not hearing. The aftershocks of the blast of the horn on our ears take a while to die off. So we sit there shouting at each other. If you were standing outside the door, you'd think a big fight was going on instead of a party.

Dad opens his presents. He loves the titanium safe.

"This is great," he says. "Let's try it out."

He reaches over and grabs my plate with the piece of cake. Putting it in the safe, he slams the door shut and locks it. He's gone crazy.

"I was eating that," I tell him.

"You'll be happy to know your slice is safe and sound. Nobody can get to it now."

"Yeah, not even me. Can't I make a withdrawal?"

"Of course. Just let me get my key."

The lock clicks and my cake reappears.

Dad adds the new key to his key ring. The ring is attached to a chain that clamps onto the belt loop on his pants. He's got about thirty keys on there, for work stuff and home stuff. He's let me hold it and I swear it weighs as much as three rolls of quarters. One time I asked him if he really needed all those keys, and he went through them one at a time and told me what each was for.

Between the three of us, we manage to polish off the entire quadruple-layer cake.

"Good cake," Mom says. "Too much of it, though."

"Yeah." Dad puts the plates in the sink. "No leftovers. Nothing to put in my safe."

"We could put my dog guides in there, and I've got some Saint Bernard hair. And that picture of me and Lynda and Leftovers in the park."

Dad snorts. "You never know when someone will try and steal our dog hair."

He picks up the safe and takes it into the living room. "Now I've got to think where to put it."

"First we need to have a little music," Mom says, putting on a CD of slow dance songs. "And I want a little dance from my big birthday boy."

Mom and Dad spin slow circles around the living room. I sit down on top of the safe and watch them go round.

Sixteen

It's pouring rain outside so we have to cut the dog walk short. Mr. Brook drops the dogs off at the doggy day care, where their owners will be picking them up soon after work. I help towel off a couple of terriers. Then we drive back to Lynda's house.

We dry off Leftovers, which isn't easy. He's really squirmy. Leftovers has this little yellow rain slicker that's too small for him. It must be Chihuahua-size because it looks like a miniature saddle on his back.

"Make sure you wipe off his feet," Mr. Brook says. "Don't want him leaving paw prints all over the house."

There's something about the smell of a wet dog, something about this rain-soaked beagle, that makes me want to run through waist-high grass with him beside me, just run against the wind and the storm, chasing each other. It's like this pre-historic feeling from when the cavemen left their caves and tamed the wild dogs to stay with them.

Leftovers charges up the stairs to Lynda's room. The dog walk was too short and he's got energy to burn.

"You leave Charlie alone!" Lynda calls, chasing after him.

"Who's Charlie?" I ask. But she's in too much of a rush.

The door to her room is open and I can hear a struggle going on inside. Lynda and Leftovers are having a tug-of-war with a stuffed animal in the middle of the room.

"Let go! Let—Bad dog!" Leftovers' jaw is clamped tight.

Finally the material gives and Leftovers comes away with a foot. Then he makes a break for the door.

"Shut the door!" Lynda yells. "Don't let him get out."

I get it shut before he can squeeze through. He looks up at me, knowing there is no escape. Lynda kneels down in front of him.

"Cough it up," she says.

The beagle spits the stuffed foot out onto the floor.

"You know Charlie is off-limits." Leftovers licks her hand. "Oh, *now* you try to play nice."

"What is that?" I ask, standing over the remains of the stuffed animal.

Lynda picks it up. "It's my stuffed monkey. Charlie the Chimp. I've had him forever." She inspects the damage.

"So why does Leftovers want to eat the chimp?"

"Because he is *so* jealous," she says, giving her beagle the evil eye. "Charlie always slept with me before we adopted Leftovers. But that dog couldn't stand it, and the first time he saw Charlie, he attacked him. Leftovers wants me all to himself."

Lynda checks to see how the foot will fit back on. "Look at poor Charlie. Look at all the times he's been stitched up. He looks like Frankenchimp."

The smile on the stuffed monkey is a little off—the two halves aren't perfectly lined up. I go up to Leftovers, lift the beagle's chin and look him in the eye.

"Maybe he had a bad experience with a monkey when he was a puppy," I say.

Lynda smiles and shakes her head. "Crazy dog." She hides the chimp in a drawer and sets the chewed-off foot beside it. "Fix you later," she tells Charlie.

While I'm crouched down beside Leftovers, I catch sight of his squeezy toy under Lynda's bed.

"There's your toy," I say, fishing it out for him. "Green Goobers was hiding from you because you're such a menace." I hand it over and the beagle lies down to give it a good gnawing.

Lynda pulls off his dripping leather ear and sets it on top of the radiator to dry.

Her room is nicer than mine. It's painted sky blue, where mine is just white. Dad says the color is really cream, but *cream* is just another name for plain old vanilla white. Lynda's got some pictures on the wall, family photo stuff. Lynda and her parents. A group shot with Leftovers in Lynda's lap.

"What's this one?" I ask. It's a picture of a whole bunch of people in suits and dresses and tuxedos.

"That's when Mom and Dad got married."

"That's a big crowd." I take a closer look. "So this is, like, your mom's family and your dad's?"

"Yeah."

I look at all the faces. "How come there's only a couple of white people?"

Lynda comes over and looks at the picture with me. "Most of the relatives from Dad's family wouldn't come to the wedding."

89

"Why not?"

"Because Mom is black. And they said it was wrong."

I'm trying to figure this out. "They said it was wrong to be black?"

Lynda shrugs. "Wrong for a black person to marry a white. Dad says they think it's wrong just to *be* black. But see right there?" She points at one of the two little white faces in the crowd, smiling in the front row. "That's my dad's mother. She showed up."

I squint up close to see the white face. The smile on the face looks real, not just for the camera.

"She comes over every Christmas Eve," Lynda says. "And other times. And she sends stuff on our birthdays. She's always saying sorry for the rest of her family."

"That's crazy," I say.

She nods. "Pretty crazy."

Leftovers squeaks a long whistle out of his toy, like he's agreeing with us.

"So I get whacked at school because I'm Whitey, and your dad's family won't see you because you're only half white." I do a big shrug. "You can't win."

"Guess not."

The beagle's toy makes a sound like a deflating balloon.

We look over at Leftovers.

"You know dogs are mostly color-blind?" I say.

We sit down on the floor with the beagle between us. Sometimes his one back leg gets sore from all the strain of holding his rear end up, so I give his leg a little massage.

I ask Lynda, "If you were a dog, what kind would you be?"

"A pit bull." She laughs. "No. Really, I'd be . . . a dalmatian. Black and white, or white and black, depending how you look at it."

"That's perfect."

I keep massaging, and Leftovers gives a happy-dog sigh.

"And you're perfect too," I tell him.

Seventeen

I'm working on a jungle. Lynda's doing a desert. We've been cutting up old *National Geographic*s for the pictures. We're doing collages in class, arranging the photos of lions and tigers and camels on big sheets of bristol board. First we have to plan it out before we get into the gluing.

Lynda's got a bunch of sand dunes she's cut out with three camels, a lizard and a trap-door spider set out on the sand. The shots of the lizard and spider are as big as the camels.

"What's that?" I ask her. "Some alien spider from Mars?"

"Could be," Lynda says. "Or maybe it's just mutated huge from all the radiation. You know, no ozone."

I move her spider so it's perched on a camel's hump. "Or maybe it had its web behind a microwave oven and got its genes fried."

She shakes her head. "I think maybe *you've* been standing too close to the microwave." She looks over at my jungle. "That's one crowded jungle. What is it, rush hour?"

I laugh. "It's wall-to-wall monkeys."

I add another cutout of a gorilla.

She points at one of my trees, where a Rastafarian guy in a rainbow-colored hat is sitting way up high.

"Who's that supposed to be?" she asks.

"That's Tarzan."

"Tarzan's a white guy," she says. "And I don't remember him having a hat."

I shrug. "This is the *new* Tarzan. He won the title Lord of the Jungle arm wrestling the old Tarzan."

Hairy Larry peeks over from the desk next door. "I like the hat," he says.

I look over at Larry's desk. He's doing the Arctic. Piles of snow and iceberg mountains, with polar bears and seals, Eskimos and snowmobiles. From a crack in the ice, half sunk, Santa's head pokes out.

"What happened to Santa?" I ask.

"Crash landing." Larry laughs.

Lynda shakes her head. "His house melted because of global warming. Because there's no ozone."

I sigh. "It's always the ozone with you."

Since it's art class, we're not chained to our desks. We're allowed to walk around the room for supplies and extra *National Geographic*s. The teacher's going down the rows, making suggestions.

Blob walks past between my desk and Larry's. He's so huge he has his own gravity, and a couple of my monkeys are blown off in the draft he makes. While I'm reaching to grab the pictures from the floor, a shoe steps on them. The shoe does a little twist, mashing the photos against the floor.

I look up, even though I already know who the shoe belongs to.

"Oh—sorry," Toothpick says, staring down at me. Then he drags his foot down the aisle with the pictures tearing apart underneath.

"Idiot," Larry mumbles at Toothpick's back.

Toothpick stops and steps back to stand behind Larry's chair. "Did the hairball say something?" he says.

Larry tries to ignore him. I try not to stare, remembering the last time Toothpick knocked the wind out of me. The teacher's back is to us; he's up by the front of the class.

Toothpick leans in closer.

Larry just stares straight ahead.

Out of the corner of my eye I see Toothpick grab something from the desk behind Larry's. I turn my head just in time to see him take a chunk of Larry's hair and cut it off with a pair of scissors.

"Time for a haircut," Toothpick says.

Larry shoots up out of his chair. He puts his hand to the back of his head and feels the bare spot. Then he sees the chunk of frizzy brown hair Toothpick's holding up.

Toothpick's smile turns to shock as Larry barrels into him headfirst, hitting him right in the gut. Toothpick grunts as he falls backward to the floor with Larry on the top of him. The teacher flashes down the row, pulling them apart, lifting Larry off still kicking.

"Enough! Enough!" the teacher tells them. "Both of you, come with me."

Larry and Toothpick get dragged off to the principal's. Everybody starts talking, reliving the fight. I pick up Larry's Arctic pictures that got knocked off when he went after Toothpick.

That's the thing about Larry, he can take any insult and shrug it off. But don't mess with his hair. Larry's got a special comb for it he always carries in his back pocket, and he's forever patting it into place.

Lynda walks down the aisle and picks up the chunk of hair.

"What should I do with it?" she asks.

"Leave it in his desk," I say. "He might want it."

When the teacher comes back, we break out the glue for the collages.

I wish I could be as brave as Larry. He never takes any crap, even though he's only about the same size as me.

"You gotta have some flash," Larry told me one time. "If you look and talk and walk like everybody else, what good is that? How you going to even recognize yourself in the mirror if you look like everybody?" He shook his head at me. "I mean, look at my hair. You ever seen hair like this? People could recognize me just looking at my shadow."

We were standing out in the soccer field, and with the sun at an angle Larry's shadow was six feet tall—and about two feet was just the shade made by his hair.

Yep. I'd know that shadow anywhere.

"You gotta stop trying to be like the Invisible Man," Larry said. "Or someday you'll look in the mirror and you won't even be there."

Eighteen

Dad wanted me to wear a tie again, but I told him I couldn't breathe with one of those things around my neck. Really, I just didn't want to give Cheryl an upset stomach, swallowing another tie. I hope she's okay.

I brought the Junkers model airplane, the last one me and Gran worked on before her stroke. I touched up the paint job last night to make it perfect.

We find Gran in her room. She's dozing in a chair by the window with the sun on her. It's an afternoon sun, so it gives her face some color, makes her look warm. When Dad touches her shoulder, she blinks her eyes open.

"Who's there? Oh, Donny. There's my boy."

Gran gives Dad and me one-armed hugs.

"I was just dreaming about you, son," she tells Dad. "I fell asleep looking out at the trees and the leaves falling." She straightens up in the chair. "In the dream you were a boy. You'd just finished helping your father rake the leaves into a pile, and he gave you a dollar to guard the pile while he got the garbage bags."

Gran smiles up at Dad. "Remember when he did that?" she asks.

Dad nods. "I remember. But it was only a quarter he gave me."

"Well, I guess he's more generous in my dreams," she says. "You stood out there in front of the pile with the biggest stick you could find, ready to scare everybody away."

Dad looks out the window at the trees. "I kept it safe, didn't I?"

"Didn't lose a leaf."

"Now you guard a bigger pile," I tell Dad.

"All seventy-seven stories of the Chrysler Building," Dad says. "I should have kept that stick."

Gran asks me, "What's in the bag?"

I pull out the Junkers. I spin the propellers and show her how the bombs detach.

"You did a great job," she says. "How about the landing gear?"

I open the small doors on the bottom and lock the wheels down into place. "Ready to land."

Gran reaches over and spins the wheels with her finger. "Pretty smooth. So what's next? You've done a B-52, a Corsair and now the Junkers."

"I was thinking. I've done the Allies and the Germans. I thought maybe I'd do a Japanese plane next."

She thinks for a second. "How about a Japanese Zero? They always used to come right out of the sun so you couldn't spot them until it was too late. Small, one-man planes. They used to attack the ships by flying right into them. Kamikaze, the pilots called themselves."

I can't believe she remembers all this stuff. If you just looked at her, you'd think she'd be pretty out of it.

"What's *kamikaze* mean?" I ask.

" 'Divine wind,' " Dad says.

Me and Gran look over at him.

"Don't look so surprised," he tells me. "Your gran taught me how to make models too. We did more artillery, though. Tanks and half-tracks."

"A B-52 can take out a tank any day," I say.

"But I also made antiaircraft guns."

Gran laughs. "Now, boys. No bombing in my room. Keath, I made you something. Over there in the top drawer."

There's a chest of drawers beside her bed. I open the top drawer and find a small white frog, made of folded paper.

"Hey, is this a new one?" I ask her.

"Just made it yesterday. That one was my fourth try."

It's not the greatest origami. The paper is kind of crumpled, not smooth like it should be, and the folds aren't totally straight. But for someone only using one good hand, this is pretty amazing.

Gran holds out her right hand and I set the paper frog on her palm. "It's good therapy for my fingers. The nurse said I should start with something less difficult, but where's the fun there?"

She hands the origami back to me. "He doesn't hop too good. Try him out."

I set it on the floor and flick the frog's rear end. It's supposed to jump forward, but this one flips on its back.

Gran shakes her head. "Nothing but back flips."

There's a commotion in the hall outside her room. We look over at the doorway in time to see a terrier flash by, followed by a wiener dog. They must be heading for the recreation room.

A woman hurries after them. "Slow down," she orders them. But you can tell by the sound of claws clicking on the floor tiles that they're not obeying.

Behind her, Cheryl rushes by.

"Cheryl!" I call out.

There's nothing for a few seconds. I hold my breath. Then her head peeks in and her sad brown eyes meet mine.

"Come on in, girl."

I kneel down and Cheryl rushes up to nudge me with her nose, knocking me back. She remembers me! I hug her neck for a long second and feel her warm drool soaking into my shoulder. She smells like an old rained-on rug left in the sun to dry.

She looks healthy. I guess the necktie went down okay. I asked Lynda's dad about that, but he said he'd seen dogs eat a lot worse. He once took care of a Pomeranian who ate half a checkerboard. Dogs don't stop to taste what they're eating, he told me; that would slow them down.

Cheryl goes over and says hi to Gran. Gran gives the Saint Bernard a little pat and gets a wet black nose pressed against her cheek in response.

"Cold nose," Gran says, reaching up with her good hand to wipe her cheek.

It's strange. I didn't really forget about Gran's left side being frozen, but I've kind of gotten used to it. It's still crunched up a bit so she looks like something pointy just jabbed her, and I remember how it used to creep me out. Now it still looks weird, but it's the same Gran inside there. And I'd rather have some of her than none of her.

Cheryl moves on to Dad. He backs up a couple of steps.

"Okay, that's close enough," he tells her. "We can say hi from here."

That's not good enough for Cheryl. She gives Dad's crotch a good sniff.

"Bad dog," Dad says. "Bad dog."

Me and Gran try not to laugh.

Cheryl finishes her examination and comes to sit beside me. She leans on me a little. If she leaned on me a lot I'd topple right over.

I tell Gran about Leftovers and the dog show. "I'll bring a picture of him next time. He's a great beagle."

Cheryl finds something on the floor and I catch her just before she tries to eat it. It's Gran's frog.

"You don't want that," I tell her. "No taste. No vitamins."

She won't take her eyes off the paper frog.

Gran waves her hand toward the chest of drawers. "There's half a bran muffin left on top there. See if she likes it."

I hold it out to Cheryl in the palm of my hand. She does a vanishing act with the muffin, then inhales the crumbs.

I go over and open the top drawer to put the origami frog back, where it can be safe.

"You keep that one," Gran tells me. "See if you can fix him, get him hopping straight."

"Okay."

I pick up the airplane model from the bed.

Opening the cockpit, I take out a piece of plastic about the size of a thumbnail. I hand it over to Gran.

"I'll take the frog," I say. "And you take the Junkers pilot."

Gran holds up the tiny figure of the German pilot and squints at it.

"I'll keep him as a prisoner of war," she says. "Confined to my drawer."

She smiles her half smile, and I give her a whole one back.

Nineteen

I always toss my dirty socks on the giant cactus in the corner of my room, the one that stands there like a holdup victim with its prickly arms in the air. But it looks bald now. It's been desocked. Mom's doing laundry.

I'm doing homework. Well, not really. I'm actually just balling up blank pages and throwing them at the cactus. My thorny plant is the closest I've ever come to having a pet. I can't touch it or play with it. I can't even water it. Mom takes care of that. It only gets to drink once a month.

I know what it needs. A hat. To give it personality.

I grab my Yankees cap, go over and stand on my

toes to put it on. I stand back, then decide the cactus would look better with the cap on backwards.

Perfect! Rebel cactus!

I ran into Mr. Kim yesterday, the man from Mom's class, wearing his ancient Yankees cap. He stopped to show me a letter he got from the *New York Post*. He's been learning how to write letters in Mom's class. So he wrote one to the *Post* about how their horoscopes are always wrong and giving them corrections.

"Their horoscope tells me I find romance on Monday," Mr. Kim said. "But it never happens. So I write and tell them Monday was rotten day. No romance, and the Yankees lose."

"So what did they write back?"

He made a face and shook the letter. "They say horoscope is written for millions of people, so it can't be right for every single person. But they don't say that in the paper. So, in today's *Post* they say maybe I find some money. We'll see what happens."

"What if you don't find any?" I asked.

"Then they get another letter from me. I'm a Leo, a lion. Leos don't take things quietly."

Then he smiled and carefully folded the letter to put back in his pocket. I think he gets more fun out of it when the *Post* gets it wrong. A lion's got to roar.

Looking at my cactus, I decide to give it some eyes. So I take two small paper balls and stick them below the band on the back of the baseball cap. They're not really lined up perfectly, but it gives the cactus more personality.

"Keath?"

I jump. Dad's at my door.

"How's it going?" he says.

I shrug. "Great. I was just . . . decorating."

"Nice touch. Is the sock look out?"

I smile. "No. Mom took them. Laundry."

Dad picks up a balled page off the floor and sticks it on one of the thorny arms so it looks like the cactus caught it.

"Not bad," he says. "It could play outfield."

I laugh. "As long as the ball is hit in the exact same spot every time."

"Still, it could use the sun."

He wanders around the room looking at stuff, stopping to study the world map tacked to the closet door.

"Got to get you a new map. Everything keeps changing. Some of these countries don't even exist anymore. New names. New borders."

I don't think Dad came to see me to talk geography. He's thinking something.

"I've been thinking," Dad begins. "About what we were talking about the other day."

I try to remember. "What? You mean about the dog show?"

Dad shakes his head. "No. Not the dogs. You were telling me about problems at school, with the other kids?"

"Right," I say. "Not all the other kids, just some. Ninety-nine percent of them."

He examines the cactus and reaches out a finger to test how sharp the spines are.

"So you've got a solid one percent that doesn't hate your guts?" Dad says.

"Pretty much." I shrug. "Actually, there's only a couple who are *really* out to get me."

Dad picks up another ball of paper and rolls it between his palms. "Who's that kid? What's-his-name, Theodore?"

"We call him Toothpick," I say. "He's the main one trying to bury me."

Dad frowns, looking out my window. I can tell he doesn't like to hear this talk about burying.

"I went to Frederick Douglass too," Dad tells me again.

"Must've been a long time ago," I say.

"Ice ages ago. Back then it didn't really have a name, except Public School Thirty-two. I had a great time there."

"I guess it was different back then."

"Guess so," he says, looking out at the street.

"The neighborhood's changed since I was a kid. It used to be mostly white, now it's mostly black. Same with your school. But kids are always kids, whatever color they are. You get good ones and bad ones. That doesn't change."

I think about Toothpick and his cracks about me being a ghost.

"Anybody ever call you Mayonnaise?" I ask. "Or Ghost?"

Dad shakes his head, walking over to my desk. "Never got any of that."

"Never got any names?"

Dad uncrumples the paper he's holding. "They called me Stretch. I was kind of tall for my age."

"But nothing bad?" I say.

"No." He flattens the paper out on my desk, trying to straighten out the folds.

"In sixth grade I had a friend named Freddie Wong," he says, leaning against the wall and crossing his arms. "A Chinese kid. He was . . . well, pretty fat. And some of the kids were brutal in bugging him about it. But the absolute worst, most rotten kid you'd never want to meet really had it in for him. His name was Dan Simmons, a white kid. He had a face like a fist, and about as much brains as a fist has.

"Dan used to say stuff like Freddie Wong ate his weight in won tons every day. You know, stupid things.

"I told Dan he was an idiot. Told him his mother must have used his head to clean the toilet, he was so ugly. Dan never came after me. I had nothing he could pick on."

"So what'd this Freddie do?" I ask.

"Well, that's the thing. There's always some loser yelling names at the other kids. The names change and the faces change, but it's all the same garbage. Usually the other kids gets crushed by the loser with the big mouth. But Freddie was different."

"How different?"

"He did this trick," Dad says. "Freddie made Dan invisible. 'Can't see him. Can't hear him,' Freddie used to say. Dan would say something like, 'Man, look at you, you're not even a Chink. You're a Chunk!'

"And Freddie would keep on talking to me about baseball or whatever like nothing happened. He didn't make like he heard at all. But I'd get mad and tell Dan off. It used to bug me that Freddie didn't fight back. But he said, 'I used to let it wreck me, but look who's saying it. Dan's an idiot. Man, he's failed two grades already.'

"It was true. The guy was an idiot. 'Even a parrot can say a name,' Freddie told me. 'But they're too dumb to know their own reflection in the mirror.'

"I said, 'So it doesn't bug you anymore?'

" 'Yeah, it does,' Freddie said. " 'But I try to remember who's saying it.'

"After a while, I just started doing what Freddie did, made Dan invisible. And that killed Dan, because he really wanted the attention."

I take the page Dad smoothed out and crunch it back into a ball.

"Did that stop him from bugging Freddie?" I ask.

"Dan still mouthed off, but since nobody was paying him any attention, it got to be like he was talking to himself."

I crunch the paper up tighter and pitch it at the cactus. It bounces off a spiny arm and falls to the floor.

"So," Dad says. "Nobody ever called me Mayonnaise or anything. But seeing Freddie get all the names and insults, I know what you're saying. I can see how it hurts. It's not easy to make the other guy invisible."

Dad tosses the paper ball back to me. "When someone starts calling you a name, what they're really saying is: 'I'm a jerk.' You know, in those foreign movies when you read the words translated into English at the bottom of the screen? Well, life should have subtitles like that. Because then, when someone says Ghost or Whitey, you could just read the subtitles and see what they're really saying: 'I'm a jerk. An idiot.' "

He pats the baseball cap on the cactus's head. "I still think it could make a great outfielder."

Dad notices the flyer for the dog show stuck on the body of the cactus. "Hey, that's tomorrow, isn't it?"

"Yeah. We shampooed Leftovers last night. He shines now."

Dad shakes his head like he still doesn't get this dog thing, but he says, "Tell the pooch good luck from me."

Twenty

I use my sleeve to wipe my cheek. I'm in the wagon-dog section of the dog show. I never knew there were so many two-legged dogs running around with their backsides strapped into customized wagons.

Shade is a black Labrador retriever. She's the one who just licked me. She doesn't drive too well—already she's run over my feet twice. None of the two-legs seem to be good drivers. They keep crashing their wagons together. It's like a demolition derby for dogs.

Me and Lynda are exploring while her mom takes Leftovers around to visit his fellow tripeds (which means three-legged creatures, Dr. Brook said).

"Look at that one," says Lynda.

She's pointing at the meanest canine I've ever seen. It's sitting with its back end in a wagon that has painted silver letters on the side.

Angel, it says. That can't be this dog's name. It must have eaten the real Angel and stolen the wagon from it. It's a white pit bull that watches the other dogs with the eyes of a hunter.

"Don't worry," says the large woman standing with him. "He can't bite you. Can't even lick you, not with his muzzle on."

The muzzle is shiny silver steel. It looks like armor.

I look over at Lynda. "Go ahead," she says. "I'll watch from here."

The woman pats her pit bull. "Say hi to your visitors now, Angel."

Angel keeps his eyes on me. I move real slow and hold out my open hand to his muzzle. He sniffs it for a full minute, then his tongue sticks out and he licks the inside of his muzzle.

"Angel says hello," the woman tells me.

"How did he lose his back legs?" I ask.

"He's had a hard life. When he was still under a year old, Angel was deserted by his owner, left chained up outside in the middle of winter. Lost his legs to frostbite."

The woman pulls a clump of loose hair off his side. "But my baby's living the good life now. You should see him speeding around the house with his wheels. He goes up and down the stairs. There's nothing he can't do.''

Angel licks his muzzle again, just managing to wet the tip of my little finger.

Me and Lynda make a grand tour of the show. There are so many sections and categories.

Deaf dogs have their own place. Almost half of them are dalmatians. A woman tells us that almost one in six dalmatians are born deaf. It's their bad genes. We visit with one-eyed dogs, even a couple of blind ones. Both of the blind ones have other dogs that guide them and herd them around.

We have a camera, so I make sure I get pictures of me with everybody. I even get one of me and Angel. He growls at the flash.

We're lost in a sea of dogs when we hear over the loudspeakers: ''The judging for triped dogs will now begin in the center ring.''

Twenty-one

There are ten dogs competing for best triped. In the ring right now, being examined by the judge, is a collie named Peepers. His front left leg is missing. He walks even funnier than Leftovers, with more of a bouncy limp.

The judge looks in the collie's eyes, feels his ears and pulls back his lips to see his teeth. Then he runs his hands down the dog's sides and checks out all three legs. The owner is standing a few steps in front of the collie, waiting for the judge to give his signal to see Peepers walk and run a little.

The judge nods. Peepers walks a few steps, then trots along beside his owner. They do a circle around the judge, and he writes numbers and notes down on his judging pad.

Next is a terrier, missing its back right leg. Then a golden retriever.

"Leftovers," the judge calls out. "Male beagle."

We're on!

Dr. Brook takes him out to the center of the ring. Leftovers is magnificent. His white belly shines in the light. His coat shines too, brushed smooth and flat.

Lynda's mom stands in front of him, four steps back. It's important to keep the dog's attention. The dog gets major points off for scratching or not staying still.

Me and Lynda are about ten feet away, facing Leftovers from just outside the judging ring.

The judge holds up the beagle's chin and stares into Leftovers' eyes. The lips are lifted up to show sparkling white teeth.

We brushed them this morning using a special dog toothbrush, which is way bigger than a human one. We also gave Leftovers some minty treats to freshen his breath. It might get him a couple extra points.

The judge goes to feel the beagle's ears, and the fake one comes off in his hand.

We forgot to take it off! Oh no!

The judge turns it around, examining it.

"Sorry," Dr. Brook says, taking it from him. "It's a prosthetic." That means it's artificial.

The judge nods and takes a close look at the ear stump.

We cleaned out Leftovers' ears, too, so the judge won't find anything bad there.

Then the judge runs his hands over the coat. Leftovers tries to look back to see what the judge is doing around his hindquarters.

He can't do that. It'll mean points off.

Luckily I have an emergency secret weapon in my pocket. A weapon by the name of Green Goobers. I give it a little squeeze, making it whistle.

Leftovers snaps to attention, looking straight forward to where I'm standing. I don't squeeze Goobers again. Leftovers would probably leap out of the ring toward me.

The judge finishes by combing the beagle's tail out to its white tip. Then Dr. Brook leads Leftovers into a short trot, circling the judge.

When Leftovers gets back to us, I show him Green Goobers and let him chew on it. We get nasty looks from some of the other owners. No squeezy toys next to the ring. It's bad manners, distracts the other competitors. So we move back and watch from a distance.

They announce the winners of the deaf and blind dogs first. Then the one-eyed.

The big surprise is for best biped (two-legged) dog.

Angel, his front end in a muzzle and his back end in a wagon, wheels into the center of the ring. A first-place medal is hung around his neck as the crowd applauds. There's no way he would have won without his muzzle on. He would have eaten the judge's hand. Second-place biped goes to a blue-eyed husky. He gets a silver medal.

And the winner of best triped goes to . . .

I hold my breath. Lynda grabs my hand. Leftovers whistles Green Goobers.

"Best triped. Peepers. Collie."

I can't believe it! What a rip-off!

"Second-place triped. Leftovers. Beagle."

We go with Leftovers to the center of the ring and wait until Peepers gets the first-place medal hung around his neck. I'm pretty mad until I look at Leftovers, who is mangling Green Goobers in a whistling frenzy.

He's happy. And this is *his* show.

So I smile, hugging the beagle with Lynda as Dr. Brook takes a photo of Leftovers getting his medal. The medal's about the size of a silver dollar, with a dog's profile on both sides instead of a president's. It hangs from a blue ribbon.

We all make our way out of the ring. When I look back and see Goobers left behind on the floor, I know something is wrong.

Leftovers has the silver medal in his mouth. It's come loose from the ribbon. Before we can get it out, he does a big swallow. Dogs never stop to taste things. Dr. Brook wrestles with Leftovers for a minute, but it's too late.

"Is that bad?" I ask.

"No," says Dr. Brook. "Not really. The medal's not too big. It'll come out eventually at the other end."

We all shake our heads at Leftovers. He goes back and grabs his squeaky toy, the blue ribbon dangling from his neck.

Leftovers leans against me, resting for a second.

"I bet first prize tastes even better," I tell him.

He squeaks Green Goobers back at me.

Twenty-two

I don't even see it coming.

Maybe it's better this way. In the movies, the guy who's going in front of the firing squad is told, "You die at dawn." So he has all night to worry about it.

Ambushed, I have no time to worry.

It's lunch at school. I'm heading to the washroom when a fist hits me between the shoulder blades and I fall forward.

I push myself up to my knees and look back. The fist belongs to Toothpick, of course. I knew that before I kissed the floor. What I don't know is why.

Not that he needs a reason. But he hunted me

down out here, alone in the hall. Usually he likes an audience, but even Blob isn't with him now.

Blob is like his traveling laugh track. Toothpick whacks somebody. Blob laughs.

"You just can't keep your eyes off me, can you?" Toothpick says.

And now I know what this is all about.

I've been avoiding him ever since he gave me that shot in the gut outside. If I see him out of the corner of my eye, I look the other way real quick. If he shoves me, I don't say anything.

But today in class he caught me watching him. Toothpick sits a couple rows over from me and two seats in front. So I didn't think there was any danger of him noticing me looking his way. I saw that his lower lip was scabbed up on one side where it had been split. It was swollen and he kept licking the scab. It looked real painful.

When I was watching, Toothpick looked up at the clock on the wall. Then he saw me seeing him. Maybe it was just my imagination, but it seemed like the black center in his eyes went a little red. I thought he was going to dive on me right there in class.

But he waited.

"Well, take a good look. Before your lights go out."

He steps toward me. I back up against the wall. I'd try and run, but there's no way to escape.

"I—I was just looking," I say. "Didn't mean anything."

How can he be so mad all the time? Why does he hate me so much?

"Shut up. This isn't a conversation."

He's talking funny with his fat lip. It makes his words slur a little. I'm betting his brother did it to him, like I saw him slapping Toothpick around before.

Toothpick gives me a shot in the shoulder, not a hard one. A warm-up.

If I could only fight back. When I went shopping with Mom, I punched the stuffing out of that pillow. I pretended it was Toothpick and went nuts. But pillows don't punch back.

Toothpick hits my other shoulder. Even his knuckles are pointy, all bones.

The door to the cafeteria swings open.

"Hey, leave him alone!" It's Lynda. She must have seen Toothpick follow me out.

"You want a smack too, Zebra?" he tells her. "Stand in line."

"Come on, man. Leave him," a new voice says. It's Hairy Larry. He's not much bigger than me. But he's still mad over what Toothpick did to his hair, and he's not scared of Toothpick anymore.

I'm glad someone's speaking up for me, but I'm just getting a bigger audience for my knockout.

"Leave him," Lynda says. She lets the door to

the cafeteria close behind her. That's a big mistake, cutting off her escape.

"Shut your mouth." He moves toward her. "Why don't you sic your stupid little cripple dog on me?"

"You shut up!" Who said that? Then I realize it was me.

Toothpick turns on me. There's this shocked look on his face. "You talking to me?"

"That's right," I say. Something is boiling inside me and the words just keep coming out.

"What's wrong? You in love with that ugly little cripple dog?"

"You're such a jerk!" I tell him. "There's nothing wrong with a three-legged dog."

Nobody calls Toothpick a jerk. He rushes at me, so I step back with my hands up to block my face. Charging ahead, Toothpick slips on the floor and falls into me with all his sharp bones and pointy knuckles.

I hear Lynda shout as I fall backwards with Toothpick on top of me. Something hits my elbow real hard, right on the funny bone, sending an electric pain shooting up my arm. I struggle blindly, expecting my face to be caved in any second.

There are a lot of voices all around, shouting. Kids are piling out of the cafeteria.

There's a weight on top of me. I feel like I'm

going to suffocate until somebody finally pulls it off and I can breathe again.

I lie there for a long second, staring at the ceiling. My head is dizzy. I raise my hand and make a fist to test out my arm, but the electric pain is already dying away.

Sitting up, I see blood on my shirt. I touch my nose and mouth to see where it's coming from.

"Keath? You okay?" Lynda says, waving a hand in front of me.

I focus on her hand. "You're making me dizzy," I say, stopping her from waving. "What happened?"

Someone is bent over, leaning on the opposite wall. My eyes unblur enough to see that it's Toothpick.

His nose is gushing blood.

"What happened?" I say again.

"You did it," Lynda tells me. "You beat him."

All the faces are looking at me. Kids from my class. Blob is there staring at me. I hear my name used here and there. Ghost. Whitey. Keath. More Keaths than Ghosts.

Didn't think they knew my real name.

A couple of kids help me stand up. One of them is Ryan, the one who slugged me a few months ago just so he wouldn't have to be the lowest worm in the class.

I have to lean on him for a second to get my balance.

"Thanks," I say.

"Yeah," Ryan says. "Hey, I didn't mean it when I hit you that time."

I'd hate to get punched by him when he did mean it. But I say, "It's okay. Just don't do it again."

One of the teachers takes Toothpick away, holding some paper towels to his nose to catch the blood. Another teacher helps me walk.

Minutes later, I'm in the nurse's office waiting my turn. Toothpick's first. I guess it's blood before bruises. I touch the back of my head, but it feels like it's still in one piece, no major bumps.

I wait with the principal until Toothpick comes out of the nurse's office. Toothpick looks away from me when he passes by. That's a change. Now *he* won't look at *me*.

They send me home with Mom. She drives me over to the doctor to get checked out, keeping one hand on the wheel and the other on my leg.

It turns out to be nothing more than a bruised elbow.

Later Lynda phones and tells me what happened. "You hit him."

"I hit him? Really?" I can't believe it.

"Well, sort of. He fell on you and his face hit your elbow. Right on his nose. There was blood everywhere. They had to mop it up."

"So I didn't really punch him?"

"I guess you could say he punched his nose on your elbow. But that still counts," Lynda says.

"Counts for what?"

"Everybody saw him. And the blood."

"Wow," I say.

"Yeah. I've never seen you so mad."

"When he said that stuff about Leftovers—I don't know, I just cracked."

"So, did they have to amputate anything?" Lynda says.

"No. Not even a Band-Aid. I just have a bruise on my arm."

"Does it look like Toothpick's nose?"

We laugh. I twist around to get a look at it. It looks like one of those inkblot tests where you see what you want to see. It could be a nose, or maybe a hippo, a purple one.

I can hear squeaking on Lynda's end of the line. "Is that Leftovers?"

"The one and only," she says.

"Does he miss me? I didn't get to scoop today."

"You didn't miss anything."

"The silver medal?" I ask.

"Hasn't showed up yet," she tells me. "Leftovers says he missed you today."

"Really?"

"He wouldn't budge when we started walking after school. Kept looking back for you. Nobody scoops like you do."

I laugh. "Yeah," I say. "I'm King of the Scoop. Lord of the Poop."

Twenty-three

When Dad gets home he comes up to my room. He still has his work clothes on, and his Chrysler Security jacket. I can hear him a mile away from the jangling of the hundred keys on the ring in his pocket.

"You okay?" he says, coming over to my desk, where I'm looking up the weight of an adult Mexican hairless dog. Thirty pounds, in case you were wondering.

"Yeah, just a bruise." I show him my elbow.

"Does it hurt?" he asks, touching it.

"Only when you touch it."

Dad moves my arm a bit, testing it out.

"Was it that Stick kid?"

128

"His name's Toothpick."

"Your mother says he's been suspended now." Dad lets go of my arm. "Maybe we should put some ice on that."

"No, it's okay. I'll live."

He jangles the keys in his pocket like he always does when he's thinking. "Maybe it's time we got you transferred to Franklin Elementary."

I'm shaking my head. "Then I'd never get to walk the dogs after school. And I don't know anybody there. At least at Douglass I have some friends."

Dad takes his key ring out of his pocket and swings it a bit on his finger. "We'll see, but things have to improve. You are *not* going to get hurt again."

He puts his other hand on my shoulder and gives it a squeeze. It's easy to feel safe when Dad's around.

When I was really little, Dad let me play with his keys and I used to go through them, figuring out or inventing what each key would unlock. There were so many, I got to thinking Dad was this Very Important Person, like things would shut down without him locking and unlocking, guarding the world. When I found out the keys were for boring stuff like offices and furnace rooms and lockers, that took some of the shine off them for me. Keys were just keys. You could get them made for a dollar each at the hardware store. But somehow it didn't matter that Dad wasn't guarding the whole world. Because he was always guarding mine.

"What are you reading?" he asks.

"Amazing stuff," I say. "This is the Mexican hairless dog. They say he's hot to the touch, because he's all skin and no fur."

"That's one bald pooch," Dad says, leaning over to look at the picture in the book.

"That's the whole point. He's Mexican hairless. He can't take the cold. It says here he's used as a natural heater on cool nights down in Mexico. People sleep with them."

"Maybe we'll get a whole flock of them. Cut down on heating costs this winter."

I laugh. I think I'm convincing him, one dog hair at a time.

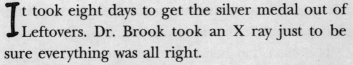

Twenty-four

It took eight days to get the silver medal out of Leftovers. Dr. Brook took an X ray just to be sure everything was all right.

"There it is." She pointed at a round white spot on the X ray surrounded by the bright outlines of Leftovers' ribs.

"Is it in a good place?" I asked.

Dr. Brook nodded. "The medal is finally exiting his intestines. And this X ray was taken about an hour ago."

Me, Lynda and her mom all turned to look at Leftovers, as if the medal might exit at any moment.

Yesterday the silver medal reappeared and Leftovers got a round of applause from me and Lynda.

Doctor Brook let me keep the X ray. I'm going to put it up on my wall. It'll make the cactus jealous, show it what a real pet is supposed to be.

It's the end of the school day and we're doing art. The last couple of days we've been studying textures, taking pencil and paper and making rubbings of different kinds of surfaces. On our table we have a brick, some sandpaper, coins from different countries and other stuff with all kinds of textures.

I like doing rubbings of the coins, because instead of Abe Lincoln or George Washington they have these kings and queens I've never heard of. There's this one Australian coin the size of a dime that has an alien-looking marsupial on it.

The class had been nice and peaceful without Toothpick. Now he's back from his suspension. Toothpick pushed past me in the hall today, but he didn't say anything, didn't even look straight at me.

Dad told me what the principal said: If you get three suspensions during the year, then you're expelled. It's called the three-strikes rule. So Toothpick is teetering on the edge—one more and he's gone. I'm hoping that means he'll forget about me. Blob still follows him around, laughing when he's supposed to.

School has been weird this last week. Some kids still call me Whitey, but even they slip and call me Keath now and then. I guess I'm not the lowest worm on the food chain anymore.

When the bell rings we scatter to grab our jackets. We have to walk by Toothpick in the hall, but he just stares right past us.

Outside, the cold air makes our breath white. The first taste of winter. Mr. Brook is waiting on the sidewalk with the pack straining on their leashes.

"Hey, kids," Mr. Brook says. "Getting chilly out. I had to make Leftovers wear his sweater."

The sweater is dark blue with stars and crescent moons on it. Looks really classy.

I give Leftovers a scratch. He leans on my leg, like he does when he's tired. I'm sort of his fourth leg sometimes, keeping him balanced. I look at the medal on his collar. It shows a three-legged dog. I search my pockets and find the stub of a pencil. Before I go home I've got to get a rubbing of the medal, to show Mom and Dad.

And maybe I can take Leftovers to visit Gran. I know she'd love him.

Looking at Leftovers with the other, four-legged dogs reminds me of this test we had last month. It was a weird test where they show you a bunch of things grouped together, like an apple, an orange, a banana and a screwdriver. Then they ask you,

"What doesn't fit in this group?" So you say, "Screwdriver."

If you look at the dog-walk pack and ask the same question, the answer would have to be Leftovers. With only one ear and three legs, he doesn't fit.

Only, Leftovers is happy hopping along on his three legs. And the other dogs don't seem to mind. So I guess he does fit, in his own way.

If you look at my class photo, you'll see my white smiling face in a crowd of brown smiling faces. What doesn't fit? If you asked me a couple of weeks ago, I would have said it was *me*. But now I don't know. Maybe I can be like Leftovers and fit in in my own way.

But I still want to be a golden retriever when I grow up.

About the Author

Graham McNamee is the author of the critically acclaimed novel *Hate You,* which was chosen as the Honor Book in the Fifteenth Annual Delacorte Press Prize for a First Young Adult Novel.

He grew up in Toronto and lives in Vancouver. He's a "book person" who has worked in bookstores, libraries and a bookbinding factory. His hobbies are drawing, photography and dogwatching.